CRYING OUT LOUD

Cath Staincliffe

severn
House

This first world edition published 2011
in Great Britain and in the USA by
SEVERN HOUSE PUBLISHERS LTD of
9–15 High Street, Sutton, Surrey, England, SM1 1DF.
Trade paperback edition first published
in Great Britain and the USA 2012 by
SEVERN HOUSE PUBLISHERS LTD .

British Library Cataloguing in Publication Data

Staincliffe, Cath.
  Crying out loud. – (A Sal Kilkenny mystery)
  1. Kilkenny, Sal (Fictitious character)–Fiction. 2. Women
  private investigators–England–Manchester–Fiction.
  3. Abandoned children–Fiction. 4. Murder–
  Investigation–Fiction. 5. Manchester (England)–Fiction.
  6. Detective and mystery stories.
  I. Title II. Series
  823.9′2-dc22

ISBN-13: 978-0-7278-8020-8 (cased)
ISBN-13: 978-1-84751-399-1 (trade paper)

All Severn House titles are printed on acid-free paper.

Severn House Publishers support The Forest Stewardship Council [FSC],
the leading international forest certification organisation. All our titles that
are printed on Greenpeace-approved FSC-certified paper carry the FSC logo.

Typeset by Palimpsest Book Production Ltd.,
Falkirk, Stirlingshire, Scotland.
Printed and bound in Great Britain by
MPG Books Ltd., Bodmin, Cornwall.

For Mum and Dad, with love

ONE

There was a baby on my doorstep.

A baby in a stroller.

One of those three-wheelers that can go anywhere.

I looked over to the gateway, waiting for whoever had rung the doorbell to appear; for some responsible adult to come sashaying up the path and make the picture right. Make my heart stop thumping. Why was it thumping? Did I know even then that something was amiss?

I crouched down. The baby was small – an infant, not a toddler. It was sleeping, its arms lying palm up either side of its head. A faint tremor crossed its eyelids; eyelids with a faint blush of blue. It wore a padded, fleecy white all-in-one with the hood up and fold-over gloves. There was a yellow blanket tucked around its legs and peeping out of the top a note, a page of lined paper from a small notebook, the bottom torn unevenly. Block capitals, blue biro: PLEASE LOOK AFTER MY BABY. DON'T TELL ANYONE. I'LL EXPLAIN LATER. 'Please' was underlined three times. Then a blurry scrawl – was it a name or just a random scribble? The beginning looked like an 'h' but the rest of it dribbled off in a wavy line. The word looked like 'henna' or 'ham'. Was it simply a slip of the pen? A fragment from a shopping list?

I stepped past the buggy and ran to the pavement; scanned the street. An eddy of wind caught a pile of autumn leaves, shed from the limes that lined the road, and whirled them round. Ghost town.

I stared at the parked cars, searching for a telltale silhouette or any hint of motion. Our house is halfway along the street, only fifty yards from the main road. I ran down there and scoured the place. The large semi-detached houses that lined the route all had that abandoned, shuttered, mid-afternoon look. People at work, at school. There was no one by the corner shop or the hairdressers next door. No one at either bus stop. The only two souls, an elderly couple, were walking towards our junction, not running away as you would if you'd just abandoned your baby. Retracing my steps, my mind was buzzing with questions. Whose baby? Boy or girl? How old? What's happened? Should I tell someone? Why me?

People hire me for all sorts of jobs: I'm a private eye. I find people or check them out; I uncover lies and track betrayals. It might be a missing son or a cheating wife, an employee pilfering goods or a gold-digger after a profitable match. I skulk about and ask awkward questions. I dig up dirt and orchestrate reunions. I don't offer childcare.

My pulse was still racing and my mouth dry. The back of my neck prickled and my guts were clenched with adrenalin. Innate responses, I imagine, to finding a lone infant. A babe alone is a frightening thing. Vulnerable. Doomed if I didn't save it. I took a breath, smelt the earthy scent of the leaves and the sweet fragrance of a neighbour's late-flowering roses. The breath of wind cooled the perspiration on my neck and at my temples. It's all right, I reassured myself. It'll be all right.

The baby was still there as I walked up the path. No mistake, no illusion. Just deal with it, I thought. Take it in. Make a cup of tea. Calm down and think it through.

There was another gust of wind; I heard the leaves on the eucalyptus at the back of the house rattle and clatter. And the bang as my front door slammed shut.

We were locked out.

Ray would be at work until teatime. We keep a spare key at the neighbours' house opposite. It was worth a try even though Jill works full-time. I wheeled the buggy round into our back garden, out of sight. The baby stirred and gave a sigh like a stutter, and for a moment I thought it was going to wake up. And then what would I do? My high anxiety gave me pause for thought, made me smile. It's a baby, I told myself, just a baby. It's not a lion or a cockroach or a snake. It won't pounce or scuttle when it wakes and you've handled a baby before, Sal – you're no novice. It had been eight years since Maddie had been born. Perspective, I admonished myself. Now find a key.

There was no answer over the road but there was one more

place I could try – the Dobsons' house around the corner, where I have a basement office. They have four daughters at various stages of teenage and young adulthood and one or other of them is often at home revising or on study leave or sometimes bunking off. The older girls babysit for Maddie, my daughter, and Tom, Ray's son. It hit me then: the second girl, Abi, was pregnant, to the disappointment of her parents who were very keen on their children getting a decent university education before starting a family. Could this be her baby? A weird quid pro quo for all the times she'd minded our kids? Had she even had her baby yet? Surely they'd have told me, a friend of the family, their sleuth in the cellar.

I couldn't leave the baby in the garden while I went round there. OK, it was asleep and out of sight, but what if something happened? I was in loco parentis – stress the loco. Besides, our garden is a haven for wildlife. I couldn't leave the baby at the mercy of the squirrels and foxes, herons and magpies.

The breeze was pushing fat white clouds across the sky and the nip of autumn was in the air. The light had that mellow, melancholy quality to it. Wheeling the buggy along the road, I felt extremely awkward. It had been years since I'd pushed a pram but more than that I felt guilty, as though someone would ambush me and ask me what the hell I was playing at. This must be what it's like when someone snatches a baby. Had this baby been stolen? Was I an unwitting conspirator in some criminal enterprise? An abduction or kidnap? I should check the news to see if there'd been any report of a baby abduction. Kidnapping was often kept quiet and off the radar. They introduce a news blackout mainly because the kidnappers always insist the police must not be involved and the police play along – it's safer that way. So if the baby had been kidnapped, how would I know? Then again, why would a kidnapper leave their hostage with me? My thoughts were getting muddled: a tangle of what ifs and maybes.

The Dobsons' house is similar to ours: a large redbrick semi built at the start of the twentieth century, with Tudor trim and stained glass. I rang the bell and studied the colours in the glass roundel on the door: ruby, cobalt and emerald, and waited for a shadow to swim out from behind them. No one came. The baby slept on.

Back in our garden, I got myself a few handfuls of water from the outdoor tap. A shock like this makes you thirsty. I sat on the patio beside the pond and gazed out at the plants, steadying myself, and let my eye roam over the Michaelmas daisies still ablaze with purple, the seed heads of the giant poppies and the eucalyptus, its grey-green leaves whipping in the wind, long strips of rusty bark peeling from the trunk.

I studied the baby's face. It had delicate and pretty features, not like those potato-head babies you see. This one had a pointy chin and a tiny nose; its skin was a creamy white, translucent over its eyelids. I watched it sleep for a few moments and saw that flickering of its eyes again. What was it dreaming of? Milk? Mummy? What do babies dream of if they haven't learnt to name the world, to navigate the world; do the dreams make any sense?

When I examined the contents in the mesh compartment slung underneath the stroller, I found a dozen nappies and a tub of baby wipes, a change of clothes and a roll of thin, slightly spongy plastic which I realized was a portable changing mat. In a padded feeding bag I found two bottles and a tin of baby-milk formula. What if the baby woke up before I got back in the house? It would be screaming for a feed and I couldn't make that with cold water. I peered in through the kitchen window. My stomach twisted when I saw that it was almost three o'clock.

We set out again and I rang Ray reverse charges from the phone box on the way to collect Maddie and Tom from school.

'Can you get away early? I'm locked out and no one with a spare key is home.'

Ray gave an exasperated sigh. Like getting locked out was some irritating habit I had developed just to annoy him.

'Or we could all just sit on the step until you get back – it doesn't look like rain,' I prodded.

'I'll leave now,' he replied, still an edge of tension in his tone. I didn't mind. While he was bound up with his own reaction to my inconvenient demands, he wouldn't pick out anything odd in my voice. I was afraid the stress was leaking out down the phone-wire. A gush of anxiety to match the gnawing sensation in my belly. If we kept talking surely it was only a matter of time before he'd pause and ask: 'Is everything all right?'

I ended the call. 'Thanks, see you soon.'

Ray has a lowly job in advertising now and it's a fairly

flexible set-up as long as he delivers the goods. We used to be platonic housemates – two single parents, a child apiece, but in the last few months we'd become lovers, to the amusement of our long-standing friends and acquaintances, my own astonishment and the despair of his mother. She had always been convinced we were sleeping together when we weren't and never missed a chance to run me down. When Ray did get seriously involved with his last girlfriend, Laura, I couldn't put a foot wrong as far as Nana Tello was concerned. But now she was back to being waspish and contrary. I was an inadequate woman with low morals and was seducing her precious son for my own ends. I was a gold-digger. I was a career woman neglecting her child to indulge in her own selfish pleasure. I was a vegetarian with all the lack of moral fibre that implied. She couched her criticisms in subtler ways when I was present, and Ray never passed on her spiky comments to me, but I had seen her in action when Laura was on the scene – I knew how it worked.

Anyway, I didn't tell Ray about the baby over the phone. I didn't have the words. It's the sort of thing you need to see with your own eyes, really. And before he arrived I wanted to decide what on earth I was going to do about it.

TWO

Maddie stopped in her tracks halfway across the playground. Then she hurtled towards me, the scowl that she usually wore after school melting away, her mouth hanging open.

'A baby,' she breathed. She thrust her lunch box at me, never shifting her eyes from the infant. She crouched beside the buggy, scrutinizing the sleeping child intently.

'See its nose.' She turned and looked up at me. 'It is *so* tiny.'

'What's that?' Tom asked as he joined us. At such a crass question, Maddie would normally have fired off a put-down with all the sarcasm an eight-year-old could muster, but she was entranced.

'A baby,' I told him. 'I'm looking after him for his mum.'

As I'd neared the school gates I'd worked on my cover story. I didn't know what sex the child was; the white clothes were neutral, ditto the yellow blanket. The buggy was a dove-grey and white design. But the change bag was blue and white stripes so I used that slim clue to christen him as a boy. I'd never bothered colour-coding Maddie when she was little. I liked the notion that people would treat her like a male child – and therefore not constrict her sense of adventure and physical boldness. According to the studies of the time, this was what happened. My attempt at social engineering hadn't been much of a success. Maddie developed into a timid girl, easily unnerved and prone to all sorts of fears. Not quite the little Amazon I'd envisaged.

'What's his name?' Tom gave the little creature a few friendly pats on the head. I winced, expecting the baby to wake, but it just gave a shudder and fluted its mouth.

'Jamie,' I ad-libbed.

'Can I push him?' Maddie straightened up.

'I want a go, too,' Tom jumped in.

'You can take turns.'

They pushed the buggy back according to a strictly-timed rota, Maddie taking elaborate care over kerbs and uneven sections in the pavement, even though the rugged design meant the vehicle could cope with rough terrain. Tom went as fast as he dared and executed a few emergency stops, a wheelie and the buggy equivalent of a fishtail spin. The infant slept on.

Ray was home when we arrived. He opened the front door, spotted the new addition and raised his eyebrows.

'He's called Jamie.' Tom was all excitement, his eyes bright as he raced to tell his dad the news before anyone else. 'Sal's looking after him. He doesn't cry or anything.'

'What, never?' Ray said wryly. He looked at me, puzzled. 'You didn't say anything.'

'I'll explain later,' I said quickly, echoing the words on the note in my pocket.

Digger, our ageing dog, strode into the hall, gave an uncertain bark and retreated back into the kitchen. Craven.

Jamie opened his eyes; they were hazel coloured. He began to twist his head this way and that, making little creaky cries.

'He must be hungry.' I grabbed the bottle and baby milk from under the buggy and held it out to Ray. 'Can you do a bottle?' He was speechless for a moment. I gave a grin; I don't think it was a convincing one – sickly, probably. Anyway, Ray took the bottle and the tin of formula, grunted and went into the kitchen.

Jamie's cries were increasing in volume and Tom pulled a face in dismay. Maddie put her hands over her ears. 'Will he stop when he's had his bottle?'

'Yes.' I hoped so. I undid the straps and lifted him up. He smelt of milk and some sort of fragrance, perhaps shampoo or washing powder, and faintly of smoke. He complained loudly as I unzipped the all-in-one and Maddie and Tom sloped off into the lounge. Jamie was wearing a lemon Babygro covered in grey teddy bears. He had a cap of fine dark hair, a longer spray of it at the front. I put him up against my left shoulder and jiggled him around, patting his back as I walked to the kitchen. There was a moment's hiatus and I thought the motion had worked, but then he started again, louder than ever. Digger got to his feet with a whine and left the room.

Ray handed me the bottle and I sat down on the rocking chair by the kitchen window. The old house has large windows which make it feel light and airy. The rocking chair, with its view out into the back garden, is one of my favourite places to sit.

'Other way,' Ray shouted and gestured as I offered the teat to the baby, whose bawling had reached desperate proportions. I'd breastfed Maddie so didn't really know my way around a feeding bottle, whereas Ray had raised Tom on his own and had done it all before. The teat looked enormous and was asymmetrical. I twisted the bottle about and slipped it into the baby's mouth. The crying stopped mid-squeal and relief flooded through me; my shoulders dropped and I took a deep breath, savouring the peace.

The baby tugged away, his eyes greeny-brown, the colour of river water, fixed on my face. Maddie and Tom gravitated back into his orbit. Now they wanted a go at feeding him but I wouldn't interrupt the baby. 'Maybe later,' I told them, 'when he's used to us.'

'How long's he here?' Maddie's voice rose with the thrill of it all.

'Not sure, probably a day or two.' I avoided Ray's gaze. He knew something weird was going on.

'Is he sleeping in our room?' Tom looked anxious – ears still hurting, no doubt.

'No, in mine,' I assured him. Ray and I still had separate bedrooms and it seemed to suit us. We were each used to having our own space and our new status as lovers hadn't led either of us to want to relinquish that.

Jamie had nearly emptied the bottle when he paused, his face creased and flushed dark red. A loud farting, bubbling sound came from his bottom.

'That is so gross!' Tom yelled.

'I can smell it – yuk,' Maddie chipped in.

'Wait till we take his nappy off.'

He drained the bottle and then I burped him, rubbing my hand along the frail bumps of his spine. More hilarity for the kids, who began a burping contest. Tom won hands down.

Ray rolled out the changing mat and brought the wipes. I extricated Jamie's legs and peeled back the tapes on the nappy. There was another chorus of groans from the kids, who were fascinated and repelled. They both moved away but not before they'd had a good look.

'Where's his willy?' Tom asked.

'You said it was a boy,' Maddie accused me.

'Did I?' I pretended confusion. 'I must be going mad. Jamie's a girl, *course* she is. I wasn't thinking straight.'

'Jamie's a boy's name,' Tom said doubtfully.

'Not always. Not this one.' I kept my head down, concentrating on the wipes. Thank God I'd picked a fairly unisex name and not Matthew or Felix or Oliver.

'Can she watch telly with us?' Maddie watched me fasten a fresh nappy on.

'Sure.'

I redid the poppers on her Babygro and took her into the lounge. There was a waffle throw there and I lay Jamie on the couch while I spread it out on the floor. Digger struggled to his feet and stalked out. The poor dog was quite bewildered by the whole palaver. I put Jamie in the middle of the waffle on her back and she made gurgling sounds. The children crowded close to her as I explained that one of them must come and get me straight away if anything happened.

'Like what?' asked Maddie.

'Like her being sick or starting to cry or you both wanting to go upstairs. Anything like that.'

'Is she going to be sick?' Maddie curled her lip with dismay.

'Hope not, but it happens a lot; they bring back some of their milk. You did it all the time.'

'Did I?' Maddie loved to hear about her life as a baby and often wanted more details than I could remember.

'Big time. Drove me mad.'

Ray was waiting for me, sitting at the kitchen table. I drew up a chair opposite him. He leant back, his arms folded, his eyes hard with suspicion. 'So, are you going to tell me what's going on?'

He listened as I recounted finding the baby on the doorstep, showed him the note and explained that I'd no idea who the infant was and therefore who had left her with me. The only person I could think of who'd been expecting a baby was Abi Dobson.

'She's still pregnant,' he said, 'I saw her at the baker's.' He uncrossed his arms and placed his hands on the table. 'We should tell the police.'

'Ray!' I protested. 'Someone has trusted me with this child. They expressly ask me not to tell anyone. Who knows what would happen if I reported it? She'd be taken into care for starters – then how hard would it be for the mother to get her back?'

'Or father.'

'Or father!' I snapped. 'Whatever. I won't do that.'

'You haven't thought this through.' He spoke as if I was one of the children.

'Don't tell me what I've thought or not thought. What are you now, a mind reader? Someone needs me to look after this baby.'

'What if it's been taken? Abducted?'

'Then why give it to me? And what kidnapper writes *I'll explain later*? If we could just work out what the signature is, it'd probably all make sense.'

He wasn't having it. 'What if she gets ill? Then what will you do?'

'That's it – look on the bright side,' I snapped.

'If anything went wrong, Sal, you'd be the one up for child neglect.'

I stood up and paced away from the table. 'Stop it. Listen, whoever it is must be in desperate straits.' Outside a black bird on the fence looked warily from side to side then flew down to the grass, stabbing its beak into the ground.

'It might be trouble of their own making,' he said. 'You've no idea what you're getting yourself into.'

'Why must you always look for the worst in people?' I complained. 'What sort of an attitude is that?' I glared at him.

'I don't,' he retorted, stung. His nostrils flared, the edges whitening. 'But when you set your mind on something you won't listen to reason.'

'You don't have the monopoly on reason. It makes perfect sense to me to look after the baby. Someone trusts me to do that. I'm not going to hand her over to the authorities.' I could hear my voice rising, my words sharpening.

'And if you've heard nothing in a week, ten days? Then what?' he demanded.

I paused and thought about my answer. The atmosphere between us crackled with antagonism. 'Then I think again,' I said as calmly as I could.

'And what do we tell people?' He still had that hard edge to his expression, his jaw muscle taut, but the question itself made me think he was coming round.

'Something simple. That I'm looking after her while her mum, an old friend, is in hospital. London: too far for visits. Surgery: a hysterectomy.'

Ray gave a derisive snort.

'What? Not a hysterectomy?' I asked. 'A car crash? No – they'd want all the details. A hysterectomy's better.'

'I never knew you were such a fluent liar.'

I was unsettled, sensing an undertone to his remark. 'I'm not, I'm rubbish. I can make them up but I can't tell them without giving myself away.'

'But you must do that at work,' he persisted.

'Not really. Not unless I'm undercover and I hate those jobs. Most of the time I just have to play things close to my chest.'

He slowly closed his eyes and shook his head. 'I don't like it,' he said quietly. When he opened his eyes again I met his gaze, taking in the way his dark brown eyes had softened a little.

'I know.' I moved to stand behind him and put my palm on his chest, feeling his heart beating, the warmth of him. He raised his hand and pulled mine to his lips. Kissed my knuckles. Again I experienced the tug of attraction that had put our lives in a spin over the last few months.

'How old do you think she is?' I asked him. 'She's not rolling over yet.'

'Search me.'

'Maybe three months?'

'She reminds me of Tom,' he said. 'The hair.'

The baby punk look. I hadn't met Ray and Tom until Tom was eighteen months. By then he was already sporting the glossy black curls of the Italian side of the family, taking after Ray's mum. Ray had answered my ad for a housemate. I was on my own with Maddie and looking for co-tenants who would be happy to share a spacious Victorian semi with a cranky two-year-old.

We'd rubbed along as housemates for almost six years, sharing the chores and childcare and growing to love each other's child, before passion had reared its head. I had been disturbed by a shocking tragedy at work and had turned to Ray for comfort. A hug led to a kiss, which pitched me into a state of uncertainty, confusion and desire, and then, after Ray had unceremoniously dropped his girlfriend Laura and set out to court me, to us being lovers. We were still adjusting to the change though Maddie and Tom took it in their stride. Nothing had really altered for them.

I wondered now whether the sudden appearance of an infant in our lives stirred up painful memories for Ray. His wife had died giving birth to Tom. Ray must have been crazed with grief in those early days – bereavement on top of the huge upheaval and the demands that a new baby brings. His mum helped out; she adored her grandson, but even so.

'It must have been hard,' I ventured, 'for you and Tom.'

'Yeah.' He rose and whistled for Digger. He'd always been crap at talking about emotions.

Ray took the dog out and I cooked tea. When I went to call the children they were balancing the remote control on Jamie's tummy and counting how long until her kicks and wriggles bounced it off. Jamie was laughing; all gums and sparkling eyes as Tom pulled faces.

There was one more hurdle to sort out before the end of the day. I waited until we had finished our pasties and apple and raisin fool. Then I took a deep breath and broached it with Ray. 'Could you work from home, tomorrow? Well, tomorrow morning.'

'You want me to look after the baby?' Quick as a flash.

'If she's still here. Just tomorrow. It's work. A meeting. I can't change things at such short notice. I would if I could. And I can't take her with me.'

'I didn't bring stuff home,' he objected. 'If you'd said on the phone . . .'

I had to persuade him to do this. I couldn't rearrange. 'Well, can't work email it to you?' I argued.

He sighed. 'Maybe. Can't you get them to come and meet you here?' he said.

'Hardly. I'm going to see man called Damien Beswick. He's in Strangeways, serving a life sentence for murder.'

He couldn't trump that.

THREE

A week before the abandoned baby materialized on my doorstep I'd started work on my new case. My client was a woman called Libby Hill. She hadn't gone into any detail over the phone but said it was an enquiry connected to the murder of Charlie Carter.

Damien Beswick, a twenty-one-year-old petty criminal, had

confessed to the murder of Charlie Carter last year. Middle-aged
Carter, who ran a loft conversion company, was stabbed to death
at his weekend cottage, in the hamlet of Thornsby, on 8 November.
Charlie's girlfriend, Libby Hill, discovered the body. The fact
that Carter was married and still living with his wife Heather
and their son added a salacious quality to some of the news
coverage. There was speculation about a love triangle and questions as to whether the murder was a crime of passion. Interest
surged when the police spent most of two days talking to Libby
Hill, but two weeks later an arrest was made. Damien Beswick
had been caught trying to use Carter's missing bank cards at an
ATM in Stockport. The next police announcement revealed that
Beswick had made a full confession. Carter had surprised him
in the middle of a burglary. Beswick, high on drugs at the time,
panicked when the older man ran at him. Beswick grabbed a
knife from the counter and in the scuffle that followed Carter
suffered a stab wound to the stomach. Arraigned at Manchester
Crown Court, Beswick pleaded guilty and asked for a number
of other offences – burglary and street robbery – to be taken into
account. It was standard practice to do that; a way of clearing
the slate so the defendant couldn't be rearrested for those crimes
on his release. Subsequently he was sentenced to life and would
serve a minimum of twenty-five years.

His guilty plea meant there was no trial by jury and the case
soon fell from public view. It was done and dusted. Justice had
been served and a violent career criminal was safely behind bars.

Libby Hill's approach was intriguing. Did she want to claim
compensation for the trauma of losing her lover? Or did she want
to make some claim on his estate, which presumably had gone to
his widow and son? Maybe it was a complaint against the police?
But when she'd come over to speak to me in person, it was none
of these issues that had prompted her to hire a private eye.

She was prettier in the flesh than she had been on the news
footage. Slightly built with fine, blonde hair caught back in a
ponytail and large grey eyes, she looked younger than her thirty-
two years. She wore faded straight-leg jeans and a blue and green
checked needlecord shirt. I'd had time to refresh my memory
about the case by trawling the Internet before we met.

We settled downstairs in my office at the Dobsons' place. It's quite comfy nowadays – a contrast to the cold, whitewashed cell I'd first rented when I set up business. I had everything I needed: broadband access, desk and chairs, filing cabinet, a bookcase full of reference books, a sofa; paintings on the walls courtesy of my friend Diane and rugs on the floor courtesy of Ikea. A couple of flight cases held my electronic equipment: camcorder, voice-activated recorder, camera and the like. I'm not big on surveillance or bugging. There are plenty of large firms out there who specialize in that sort of work for corporate clients. My work is more personal, domestic, intimate. I prefer it like that.

I made Libby a drink and assured her that there was no charge for an initial meeting. She needed to assess whether I was the right person for the job and I needed to decide whether it was something I was willing to take on.

'I read about the murder,' I told her. 'I'm sorry. It must have been terrible.'

She nodded. 'Still is, actually. You keep wondering when life's going to return to normal. I don't know if it ever will. When I think of Charlie that's how I see him; that moment – finding him – that's the first image that comes into my head. It dominates, you know? I hate that.' She spoke calmly, though her voice trembled a little at the end and she shook her head as she finished speaking.

'Anyway.' She slapped her palms on her knees, nails French manicured, hands slender and pale against the washed-out denim. 'I got this about a month ago.' She lifted her suede shoulder bag on to her lap and unzipped it. She drew out a small envelope and handed it to me. Libby's name and address were handwritten but the folded sheet inside had been done on a printer and a couple of words had been misspelled.

14 Leeson Close
Northern Moor
Manchester
M23 JIB

Dear Miss Libby Hill,
    My name is Chloe Beswick. I am Damien Beswick's half-sister. I am sorry about what happened to Mr Carter but

there is something you should know. Damien told me he didn't do it and that he only confessed because it was the easiest thing to do. Damien is a drug user and has lots of problems and he was confused when they interviewed him. When he told me I went to his lawyer but she said there was nothing she could do unless their was new evidence.

I believe my brother and their has been a miscarriage of justice. It also means the person that did it is still free. I am sure you want the right person to serve time for this. If the police and the brief will not look for new evidence then I don't know how to get a retrial for Damien. Maybe I will have to do a campaign.

Yours faithfully,
Chloe Beswick

When I'd finished reading the letter I looked across at Libby. 'This must have been a shock.'

'You got that right.' She gave a sharp nod. 'I don't know why she's written to me. I don't know what she wants.' A frown creased her brow.

'No, it's not clear. Perhaps she just wants to let you know, to warn you, that she has doubts about the conviction and that she might start this campaign, as a sort of courtesy. Did she write to Heather, too?'

'No idea. We're not exactly on speaking terms.' Her grey eyes flashed.

'No, of course, I'm sorry.' I should have realized. I felt a little clumsy, and hoped she wouldn't doubt my competence.

'It's a bloody cheek,' she said. 'You know what I think – he's finding it hard in prison so he's clutching at straws.'

'There was other evidence used to convict him as well as his confession?' I checked.

'Too right.' She placed one index finger on the other, prepared to count off the items. 'They could place him at the cottage; he'd taken Charlie's wallet.' Her face tightened. 'And there was blood on his trainers.'

Pretty damning stuff. 'The CPS wouldn't have gone ahead with the prosecution if they didn't think they had solid grounds,' I told her. 'On the other hand, mistakes do get made.'

There had been a number of high-profile cases in the last few years: Stephen Downing, a teenager with learning difficulties who confessed to the murder of Wendy Sewell in Bakewell and had served twenty-seven years behind bars before having his conviction quashed; Stefan Kiszko, bullied into confessing to the sexual assault and child-murder of Lesley Moleseed was finally freed after sixteen years, years during which the real killer continued to abuse children; and Barry George, a mentally-ill man convicted on the basis of a single particle of gunpowder in his coat pocket, served eight years for the murder of TV presenter Jill Dando before being freed at retrial.

'And sometimes people make false confessions,' I added. 'I don't know how often – I suppose that's difficult to establish. You can only know it's a false confession if you disprove it – or someone else steps forward.' I looked at her. 'What do you want me to do?'

'Find out what the hell they're playing at,' she said frankly. 'Talk to this sister, talk to him. Maybe it's some sort of scam. If it is, I'll report them.' Her brow furrowed; her thin face was taut, containing frustration. When she spoke again her words were clipped, her tone intense. 'He confessed; he was convicted. It's been hard enough to cope with as it is. But this . . . this is way out of line.'

Before I spoke to either of the Beswicks, I needed to have as comprehensive a grasp as possible of the background to Charlie Carter's death. Without a trial there were no transcripts to help so I would have to rely initially on what Libby could tell me. I asked her to start with their relationship.

'It'd been going on for over a year by then,' she said. 'I'd first met Charlie when he came to give me an estimate for a loft conversion. I run a marquee hire business. We've an industrial unit where the tents are stored and checked in and out. I'd an office there but it was a miserable place to work.' She grimaced. 'On my own most of the time and the place was freezing – no natural light. With the computer and mobile phone there was no reason I couldn't run things from home. I'd still be going out on site visits and organizing the lads for set-ups and strikes.'

I frowned; I didn't understand the reference to strikes. I repeated the word.

'That's what we call it when we take them down – comes from the circus, I think. But the rest, the invoicing and dealing with calls, I could do anywhere.'

'OK. It's your own business?' I encouraged her to continue and made notes as she talked, capturing facts and figures and the gist of her story.

'Yes. My dad started it off in the eighties and I helped out. When he died I carried it on. So, Charlie came and gave me an estimate for doing the loft. He wasn't the cheapest but I liked some of the suggestions he made, and the fact that he did the work himself. I wouldn't be faced with two contractors I'd never met and all the risk of crossed wires and them cutting corners. Long story short: by the time the loft was finished we'd fallen for each other. I knew his situation – he was totally honest with me.'

'How did he describe it?'

'That he was married; they had Alex. He wasn't desperately unhappy but he didn't think he and Heather would stay together in the long run, though she would probably want to.'

I'd already formed an impression of Libby. I believed her for a start; she was honest, direct. She had an energy about her, focused, contained and I could imagine her being practical and always busy.

She placed her hands on her knees again. 'I'd never thought I'd date a married man. Seemed like a mug's game. Plus he was a fair bit older than me – thirteen years between us. He was no oil painting, either,' she smiled, 'beer belly growing and his hairline shrinking, but we saw each other a couple of times a week throughout that summer. In the November we had our first weekend away – Venice.' She paused, her grey eyes growing distant as she picked through the memories. 'By the following summer, last year, we both knew it wasn't just a fling.'

'What was he like?' I asked.

She took a deep breath and exhaled with the weight of trying to sum him up. 'He made me laugh. We laughed so much. He'd a real quick wit; he could see the daft side of anything. And he'd clown about, too. Ring me up and put on funny accents, spoof emails.' She thought for a moment, her head craned to one side, her hand stroking her ponytail absent-mindedly. 'He was a very kind man – nothing was too much trouble. The number of times he'd be late because he'd helped someone who'd broken down or he'd run an errand for a mate – that sort of thing. Good company. Some men, they're tense, wound-up, you know?'

I thought of Ray, who was exactly like that given half a chance. 'But Charlie was pretty laid-back,' she went on. 'The only time I ever heard him get steamed up was in the car. If we got stuck behind a tractor or some Sunday driver then you could see the steam coming out of his ears. He was like a different man in the car. He'd overtake when there was barely room to get a bike past. Nerve-shattering. I hated driving with him.' She paused. 'He was bloody brilliant,' she added, her voice creaky and her eyes glistening. She blinked hard and looked down at her hands, rubbing at the polished nails. I felt the lurch of sympathy.

'So.' She cleared her voice. 'We talked about wanting to be together and Charlie said he didn't want to leave until Alex had finished high school. It would mean waiting another nine or ten months and he asked me if I'd do that.' She gave me a sideways glance. 'No-brainer. Charlie already had the cottage by then. He and Heather got it as an investment property. It didn't even have a roof when they first bought it. They were doing it up to sell on. Then Charlie thought it might be somewhere for us, eventually. Heather could keep the family home and he'd take the cottage. I wasn't sure whether I wanted to give up my little house. I'm a city girl – Manchester's the only place I've ever lived – but in the meantime we could use it as a getaway. That was the plan. Then Heather found out about us,' she said flatly. 'I don't know what made her suspect but she checked his phone.'

'When was this?' A prickle of suspense spread down my back.

'Last October. First I knew he rang me at work. They'd spent half the night talking; Charlie'd told her he was leaving and she was devastated.' Libby winced. 'Heather agreed they needed to keep it from Alex until his exams were over. But she made Charlie promise not to see me in the meantime. He accepted. So there was this awful charade going on: them sharing a bed and me in purdah.'

Jealousy is a powerful motive but I assumed Heather had a firm alibi or she'd be a prime suspect. I asked Libby about it.

'Rock solid,' she answered me. 'I never knew the ins and

outs – the police don't tell you everything – but she was with a friend, Valerie Mayhew.'

'Were there any other suspects?'

'Apart from me?' she sounded bitter. 'No.' Then she hesitated and backtracked. 'Though there was a guy that Charlie had been in business with: Nick Dryden. He was a piece of work – had his fingers in the till for months, apparently. When Charlie found out he pursued him through the civil courts but Dryden declared himself bankrupt and Charlie never saw a penny. Dryden climbed into a bottle and lost his wife, his kids, his home. The crazy thing was he blamed Charlie. He was the only person I ever heard Charlie slagging off. But that all happened six, seven years ago. Ancient history. I think he went to Spain.'

'So, you never met him?'

'No – before my time.'

'And you were a suspect?'

She hesitated. 'Yes, I'd found Charlie. And they had to "rule me out of their enquiries", as they put it. They went over and over the same ground. Had we rowed? Did Charlie decide he was staying with his wife? Before they interview you, they ask you these medical questions so I had to tell them I was pregnant and they tried to use that.'

I looked across at her, startled. 'Really?' It was a fact I'd not come across in any of the media reports.

'Had we argued about the baby? I told them time and again that Charlie didn't even know about the baby.' Her voice began to shake. 'That was why I arranged to meet him; it meant he'd break his promise to Heather about not seeing me but I was desperate to tell him about the baby. I'd only done the pregnancy test that week. It was a total surprise – an accident really, but I was over the moon and I knew Charlie would be as well. The baby was due in June and by then the whole mess would be sorted out. We'd be together.' She sighed and leant forward, bracing her arms. 'If I'd only got there earlier,' she said quietly. 'Saturday's always a big day at work: weddings and parties and festivals. Although we get the tents up on Friday, so there's plenty of time to dress them, there can be last-minute glitches. I'm on call most of the day. Then I've errands to run: the dry-cleaners, grab something nice to eat. I was supposed to be at the cottage around five but when I knew that was pushing it, I texted Charlie to say I was running late. It was just after six when I got there.'

She rubbed at her face and took a deep breath. She looked straight at me, her grey eyes stark with emotion. 'And it was too late.' There was a tremor in her voice. 'He never knew about Rowena, our baby, and she never met him. So this . . .' she pointed at the envelope, '. . . please just find out what the hell they think they're playing at.'

FOUR

That first night with baby Jamie was terrible. Enough time had elapsed since Maddie was born for the memories of looking after an infant to become smudged and hazy. And Maddie was *my* baby. This was a stranger and that added to my anxiety.

Even though Jamie slept for three hours after an eleven o'clock feed, I didn't. As soon as I turned out the lights the worries crowded in on me. What if Ray was right? What if something happened to her while she was in my care? Cot death! I snapped my bedside light back on and checked that she was still lying on her back. The room was cool but I got out of bed and opened the window a little wider. Back between the covers, I turned the light off and tried to distract myself by concentrating on what I wanted to get out of my forthcoming meeting with convicted killer Damien Beswick.

I couldn't hear Jamie breathing. Dread stole through me. I turned the light back on and crossed to the travel cot that I'd borrowed from the neighbours across the road. Peering closely at her chest, I held my own breath, as if stilling my body might magically animate hers. And it did. An almost imperceptible shift – so slight that I had to measure the movement by contrasting the motion of the popper on her Babygro with the static pattern of yellow ducks on the navy material of the cot.

Jamie jerked in her sleep, her arms flew akimbo and her eyelids fluttered open. Startled, I almost squealed as the kick of surprise shot a spike of adrenalin into my heart and sent tendrils of it snaking down my back.

It was ridiculous. She slept on, her eyelids slowly closing and her mouth moving in an imaginary suckle. But I was shot to pieces. Too tense to sleep, I sat up in bed and opened my book. But even the magic of Kate Atkinson couldn't soothe my chattering mind. *I'll explain later.* How much later? I had half expected the doorbell to ring while we were having tea. A friend or acquaintance to be standing there, apologizing for the melodrama, explaining how she'd been taken ill and had to get to A&E, or how her baby-minder had cried off and she was desperate for that interview.

But of all the excuses I could think of, nothing really seemed plausible. What would drive you to abandon your baby without explaining at the time? How long would it have taken to tell me what was going on? Another five minutes. Why so cloak and dagger? Ringing the bell and disappearing before I could see her. She'd had time to write a note, time to pack nappies and formula, so there had been some foresight.

Where was she now, the mother? Awake somewhere, fretting about her baby? Sick with anxiety, fearful that something might have gone wrong? Struggling with the enormous pain of separation? The baby was so small, so young and still at an age where it's hard to separate mother from child: physically, emotionally still bound together. When Maddie was that tiny I'd been overtaken by a dark, panicky and crippling sense of looming disaster whenever she was away from me, even for an hour or so. Perhaps it's a response hardwired into us to keep us caring for our young ones, or maybe I was a bit paranoid, or depressed, struggling on my own with a patchy support network and coping with my first baby. Whatever, I couldn't imagine Jamie's mother was resting easy tonight.

A dozen nappies; we'd already changed Jamie twice. At a rate of six a day there was enough for two days. Was that significant? Would her mother be back then? But there was only one change of clothes – which suggested she hadn't planned to be gone so long.

The questions came at me all night long; a perpetual quiz with no answers. When I did drift off, just before three, Jamie woke up, crying for a feed. No doubt there are devices you can buy to keep a night bottle warm but we hadn't got them. Instead I was forced to try mixing a bottle while I jiggled her on one arm and felt the cold steal round my ankles and my neck.

I fed her in bed. My eyes were dry and tired and I closed them as much as I could. She became dozy towards the end of the feed and I was tempted to just lay her back in the cot but her nappy felt heavy and damp and was starting to leak out of the edge on to her clothes. I winded her first, the air escaping in a watery gurgle. I wondered if her crying had woken Ray and wished he was here giving me some moral support. Highly unlikely given his objections to the whole enterprise.

Jamie complained when I wrested her out of her Babygro – not loudly but the night was silent and so every noise was magnified. It's rare that things are so quiet in south Manchester, with the trains passing quarter of a mile away, the roads busy, aeroplanes in the day and, most of the year round, students having fun late into the night. But this night was still. The city slept. Even the wind was resting.

Nappy changed, I remembered the old trick of putting my fists through the Babygro and drawing it over hers. The jumpsuit was barely damp and would last till morning.

'There we go.' I lifted her up, her face level with mine. She smiled and for a moment there was a connection there, person to person; for a moment she wasn't a puzzle or a burden or a cause for concern, but a little human being smiling at me.

'Back to bed.' I drew her close and moved to the cot. She convulsed once and threw up all down my neck.

And I tell you this – way more liquid came out than ever went in.

Night bled into day and by then Jamie was wearing a hastily adapted roll-neck T-shirt of Maddie's in black and white stripes. Très chic. The kids got up at seven thirty and joined us in the kitchen, followed shortly by Ray.

'Did you hear her?' I asked him.

'Loud and clear.' He clattered around, pouring muesli and slicing bread. A small, irrational part of me resented the fact that he had left me to it. That he hadn't sought me out and shown a bit of solidarity. But I understood the way he worked, too. Ray saw this as my problem; he thought I was handling it the wrong way so he would stand well clear, palms front, arms out to the side in a hands-off gesture and watch me sink or swim, eager for an 'I-told-you-so' opportunity.

I was still amazed and very grateful that he had agreed to look after her while I went to the prison.

'Like the outfit.' He nodded at Jamie's stripes.

'My new range,' I said. 'We need to get her some more clothes. She was sick over her spare set. They might have some in the charity shops.'

He gave a sigh. 'Anything else?'

'No, that's all. If you can't find any, text me and I'll call somewhere on my way back.' There was a Children's World in Ancoats en route from the prison.

'When's your meeting?' He buttered toast.

'Nine thirty. I can take them first.' I nodded at Maddie and Tom, who were trying to get Jamie to talk.

'And when will you be back?'

I began to clear the table. 'Say about one to be on the safe side. There's often a lot of waiting about.'

I was fibbing, buying time so I could fit in a bit more work before taking over from Ray. It was fair to assume that he wouldn't be prepared to look after the baby any more; he'd only agreed because it was an appointment I couldn't reschedule. I'm a lousy liar so the table clearing meant I could avoid his eyes and mask any increase of colour in my cheeks.

'I want to hold her,' Maddie said.

'Does she like Crispies?' Tom asked Ray.

'No, she's too little. Just baby milk for now,' Ray told him.

Jamie gave a gummy grin and Tom yelled with laughter.

'You two: do your teeth and get your bags ready,' I said.

'When's she going home?' Maddie asked. 'Can she stay the weekend?'

'We'll see.'

When the children had gone upstairs, Ray stooped and picked Jamie up. He ran his hand across her head, stroked her baby quiff then cradled her skull in his palm. I loved the sight of them like that: the baby so tiny next to him, his easy confidence as a

carer; Ray's dark curls, the stubble peppering his jaw, his moustache contrasting with the baby's soft smooth skin.

'What if the mother shows up while you're out?'

'Get her to call me.' I thought again. 'No, I can't take my
mobile in with me. Don't let her leave without a good explanation. I want to know who she is and where the fire was. And it
had better be good!' I tried for jokey but he wasn't amused. As
for me, the night had taken its toll and I was becoming more
edgy about the baby.

Driving towards Strangeways later that morning to see Damien
Beswick, I reran my visit to his sister Chloe, almost a week
earlier. She had been my first port of call once I'd agreed to look
into the case for Libby.

Chloe worked on the tills at the big Asda supermarket in
Wythenshawe but was at home when I called her on the phone
to arrange a meeting. At first she seemed to think I was offering
to run the campaign for her brother's release. It took me a couple
of goes to explain who I was and my role in it all. Chloe spoke
quickly with a flat Mancunian accent, tinged with the cultural
twang that the nation's urban youth seemed to have copied whole-
sale from young black kids.

'Yo better come 'n see us, then. Yo got the address?'

Leeson Close was on the council estate to the north of
Wythenshawe Park. Taking the road which skirted the park, in
the shade of the large forest trees, I spotted more signs of autumn.
The silver birch leaves were already yellowing and the big bunch-
of-five leaves on the chestnuts were curling and crisping. Many
of the chestnuts were sick, their familiar conkers not developing
and there was talk of a virus, like Dutch elm disease, at work.
It was a still, bleak day. Clouds grey as dirty linen muffled the
sky and the threat of rain hung brassy in the air.

Chloe's house was a simple semi-detached, brick built, dating
from the post-war years. It had been refurbished with double-
glazed windows in stubby plastic frames and a new roof. The
front garden was tarmacked and a lone black and white wagon
wheel, like a prop from a pioneer western, leant against the front
wall; the only adornment.

Chloe opened the door with a baby on one hip and a toddler

at her side. She led me into the living room, placed the baby on a play mat and told the toddler, a little girl in pink tights and a purple dress, to watch the telly. A Charlie and Lola cartoon was on and the child settled happily on her tummy a few inches from the screen, her chin on her hands, angled up at the telly. It was a flat screen with a group of dodgy pixels at the left-hand side and a yellow cast to the colours.

The room was cool and sparsely furnished. A shiny sofa slumped against the back wall and there was a bamboo coffee table and in one corner a PVC box of toys.

The kitchen was off the sitting room and Chloe left the door open so she could hear the children. She didn't offer me a drink, as most people would do, but sat and waited for me to talk.

Chloe had incredibly pale skin, almost translucent, and large pale ginger freckles across her forehead and cheeks. She wore thin black eyeliner which made her look hard, mean even, and pink frosted lipstick. Dressed in a close-fitting navy vest and trackie bottoms, with an open zip-up hoodie in red, she had painted her nails to match her lips but her fingers were stained nicotine yellow. A tattoo of a butterfly nestled in the hollow of her throat. She toyed with a throwaway lighter.

'Tell me about Damien.' An open-ended question to get her started.

'He's my half-brother: same dad, different mam. He came to live with us when he was about eleven. She'd gone off the rails, his mam.'

I looked at her for more.

'Druggie.' She shrugged. 'She did some time. Damien never went back.' She turned the lighter over and over, marking time to the story.

'Is she still around?'

'Nah. She went down south, someplace. No one knows how to find her. She dun't know he's inside, prob'ly dun't care. Damien breathes trouble – he's no sense. Not wicked just . . . dense, innit.'

I kept my face straight at the 'innit', though it always sounded such a parody to me after being lampooned by so many comedians. Would Maddie start using it when she reached her teens? Or the equivalent slang for her time? No doubt.

'We had the police round day an' night. Robbin', dealin',

burglary, possession. Gets to the point where my dad kicks him out for good.'

As a character reference it was pretty damning. 'How long ago?'

She watched the lighter, took a breath and calculated. 'Six years. He was fifteen, I was twelve.' Which made her eighteen now – and the mother of two.

'Damien was getting well out of order. And there was the little ones: I've twin sisters. And me mam – she's had enough of him.'

There was a clunking sound, a hiss of static; the light went off and the sound of the telly cut out. The toddler began to cry.

'All right, babes,' Chloe yelled out, 'just the lecky. We'll go to the shop in a bit, yeah?' She turned to me, her face flat and drained of emotion. 'Fiver doesn't last five minutes in this thing.'

'They reckon it's the most expensive way to pay,' I said.

'They're right there, innit.'

'So Damien was already well known to the police?' I said. 'And did he get into more trouble?'

'All the time, 'cos of the drugs. But low level, you know? Least till last year but by then he was using a lot of coke and it wasn't doing him any good. If he could only have kicked that . . .' She left the sentence unfinished.

'And when he confessed to the murder?' I asked her.

She shook her head. 'I din't believe it. He's not a hard man. He's never been done for assault, let alone aggravated.' I knew the jargon – 'aggravated' meant a weapon was involved. 'Damien never got into fights. Too busy fighting himself.'

'How d'you mean?'

She picked up the lighter and tapped it against her palm. 'He's his own worst enemy. He lives in some fairy land half the time, innit. Living it large, showing off, giving it the gab, kidding himself that he's the man and things are fine. People buy into it, then they find out it's make-believe and they get mad. Next thing he's a headcase, crying like a baby and it's the end of the world. He's got mental problems.' She glanced across at me. 'He reckons the drugs help, but they just make it worse.'

I was impressed at the sketch she conjured up. She'd obviously thought about her brother, considered his behaviour and her analysis was unflinching.

'Why would he confess if he hadn't done it?'

She rolled the wheel on the lighter; the flint sparked but no flame caught.

'I don't . . .' She broke off, considering how to explain it to me. 'It's just the sort of thing he'd do.'

'But it must have been plausible for the police, for the judge, to accept his plea.'

She locked eyes with me, an edge of resentment hardening hers. 'He's a good liar,' she said baldly. 'That's what I'm sayin', innit. He mixes it up: what's true, what's not.'

'So you never believed it, not even when he was sentenced?'

'No way.' Her mouth flattened a firm line.

'And since?'

'I'm the only one who visits,' she said. 'The rest, they've no time for him. Mostly we talk about other stuff but then one day, he's been in about a month, he's all quiet and he says he didn't kill Mr Carter and it's a mistake and he only confessed because he was scared and he was rattling . . .'

'Rattling?' What did she mean?

'Withdrawal. So he said yeah he done it and then it was hard to go back.'

I must have seemed sceptical because she sat back and looked away in a gesture of thinly veiled frustration. 'Don't take my word,' she said, 'go see him.'

'I will. Chloe, you wrote to Libby Hill – what about the Carter family?'

'Yeah, them an' all. I went to the lawyer but she was no use. Just said I was wasting my time and there was no new evidence.'

'Did the Carters get in touch?'

'Nah.' She shook her head, resignation on her face. 'Guess they don't wanna know.'

We swapped details so she could arrange to get me on the list for a prison visit and the toddler wandered into the kitchen and climbed on to Chloe's lap. The child's face was flushed, her eyes large and drowsy. She laid her head against her mother's chest. Chloe picked a soother out of the raffia tray on the table, sucked it clean and slipped it in the little girl's mouth. 'There y'are.'

'Nap time.' I smiled.

'Thank God,' said Chloe. 'She's been up since four
– teething.'

'I can see myself out.' I got to my feet.

She nodded. 'When you see him, don't let him muck you
about. He's a bit ADHD, you know.' Attention deficit hyperac-
tivity disorder: unable to concentrate, unable to sit still, disruptive;
an increasing diagnosis among both kids and adults, many of
whom were tranquilized to settle their behaviour. It was common
knowledge that food additives played a part; I wondered what
they fed people like Damien in prison.

'Just don't let him arse you about,' she said.

I smiled. 'OK, I'll do my best.'

I wondered if Damien Beswick had any idea what Chloe was
trying to do for him. Against all the odds, knowing his flaws,
she was sticking up for him, believing in him. It seemed she was
the only person in the world who did. Whether that belief was
justified was a completely different matter. And it was my job
to start snooping around and find out.

FIVE

S trangeways is just north of the city centre, a couple of
minutes' drive from Victoria train station. The tall watch-
tower is Italianate in style, a landmark I could see as I
drove closer. It's a familiar feature of the city skyline. The building
is Victorian Gothic – red and cream brick, and the main entrance
boasts two rounded towers and steeply pitched roofs. The prison
was designed by Alfred Waterhouse, the same man who had done
Manchester's town hall. Strangeways is a panopticon design: the
wings run off from the central vantage point – like spokes from
a wheel.

They don't actually call it Strangeways any more; it was
renamed HMP Manchester in the wake of the riots that destroyed
most of the original buildings. The worst riots in the history of
the penal system. On April Fool's Day, 1990 it all kicked off. A

group of prisoners had decided to accelerate their protest against inhuman conditions: the rotten food, men held three to a cell (cells twelve foot by eight and built for one), the degrading business of slopping out, the lack of visits, of free association, the racism and brutality of many guards. The ringleader, Paul Taylor, spoke after Sunday morning's chapel service and when guards intervened, the prisoners got hold of some keys. Taylor escorted the chaplain to safety and then declared it was time for some free association. It lasted for twenty-five days. The leaders of the riot spent much of the time up on the high rooftops, communicating with the press and waving clenched fists for the photographers on board the helicopters swooping above them. Iconic images.

I remember the sense of dread and panic as the early reports came in: stories of prisoners being torn apart, of twenty dead, of people burnt alive, of hundreds of inmates breaking into the segregation unit where the paedophiles and informers were held, hauling them into kangaroo courts where summary justice was doled out, victims castrated and dismembered in orgies of operatic violence. The men on the roof had hung out a home-made banner: a sheet with the words *No Dead* daubed on it. Among the clamour of moral outrage and lurid speculation one or two more measured accounts were heard; the local journalists built up a rapport with the protesters and made every effort to give an accurate account of events. There was great sympathy for the prisoners' cause in the city and beyond. And the eventual truth was that two men had died. Both in hospital, not in the prison: a prison warder who had suffered a heart attack and a man on remand for sex offences who had been beaten. No one ever stood trial in either case. The prison was effectively destroyed and when it was rebuilt along with the new name there was a change in conditions.

The visitors' centre is a new building close to the car park up the hill near the old Boddington's brewery. At the gate I signed in, showing my passport as proof of identity. I left my bag and phone in a locker, put my paper and pen in a tray for examination and went through the metal detectors. A prison officer escorted me through two sets of locked gates and into the centre.

No matter how many times I visit prison, I never get used to the particular atmosphere. It's a combination of oppressive loneliness and boredom tinged with hopelessness and the threat of violence, all covered in a thin veneer of normality. A third of men inside have serious mental health problems, a quarter are drug dependent, a third alcoholics, illiteracy is rife and most of them come from broken homes. Lock a load of people like that up and the vibe is never going to be great.

As mine was an official rather than a social visit I could meet Damien Beswick in one of the small rooms set aside for such encounters. The prison officer left me there while he went to fetch Damien. When he brought him in, I caught the tail end of a lecture. The guard sounded weary, as if he'd been repeating something incessantly.

'Any fun and games and you lose your privileges. Governor's report.'

'I know,' Damien replied.

'I'll be right outside,' the prison officer told me.

Damien Beswick shared the same pale skin as his sister and the freckles too, but his were darker and he had collar-length black hair, thick sideburns and bushy eyebrows. These combined to give him a simian look, an impression strengthened by his physical restlessness. Even as he took his seat, he was shuffling about, fingers tapping on the table, eyes glancing this way and that. I went to shake hands and he gripped mine then quickly let go.

'Chloe told you I was coming?'

'She said Mr Carter's girlfriend asked you to come,' he replied. 'You bring anything with you?' His face was hungry. 'It's tight in here,' he went on, 'people steal your baccy—'

'Sorry, no.' I cut him off. 'But I'll ask Chloe for you.' Tobacco remained the most popular currency inside.

There was a flash of disappointment on his face. He drummed his feet on the floor, then twisted in the chair. 'I didn't do it,' he said rapidly. 'I never killed him.'

'But you confessed.'

'Yeah, but I was . . . Look, they caught me with his cards. I'd been there, at the house, couldn't say I hadn't, but that was after. He was already . . . you know.' He looked about, cast his eyes up to the ceiling. Why so coy?

'How do you know?' I asked him.

'What?' Mouth slack, startled by the question.

'How do you know he was dead?' I said.

He sighed and shook his head. 'It's not easy, talking about it.' Then his mood shifted; he was suddenly lively. 'You ever seen a dead person?' Like an excited schoolboy, eyes alight.

'Yes. But we're not talking about me.'

'You don't believe me,' he protested. He pushed back in his chair as if hitting out at it.

'I haven't exactly got a lot to go on yet.'

'This guy on D wing,' he said, 'he's the same – got fitted up. Was his auntie that died and he was gonna get the house and everything so the police, they—'

I remembered Chloe's warning: *Don't let him arse you about.* 'Let's stick to your story, Damien. Tell me what happened, everything you can remember, from the beginning. How did you get to Thornsby? Why were you there?'

'You see that?' He held his hand out. It was shaking. 'Takes for ever to see the doctor. I need something to calm me down. You can't just cut off a supply like that; it's not right.' It was exasperating: he was avoiding my questions, wanted to talk about his drug problem. We were wasting time.

'Did you get the bus?'

'They chucked me off at Thornsby. It was dark already. It was freezing. I'd been over in Sheffield. I just needed to get some readies, swear on my mother's grave.'

'Dead, is she?'

He grinned, caught out. His face lit up, his teeth were white and even, his smile broad. It transformed him. Then his expression clouded. 'Might as well be,' he muttered.

'The cottage . . .' I prompted him.

'There's a car outside but no lights on in the house, nothing. That's asking for it. When I try the door, it's not even locked. Inside, I can't see a thing. I use my lighter.' Damien looked down. 'He's there, just lying there, blood on the floor.'

'Did you touch him?' I could hear doors clanging in the prison somewhere and sporadic shouts.

'Yeah, his pockets. Nothing. Then I saw his wallet on the counter. I took it, legged it. That's all.'

'Then what?'

'Waited for the bus. They're every half hour.'

He seemed callous, indifferent.

'And you didn't tell anyone? Didn't think to report it?'

'Wouldn't have helped him,' he said sullenly.

How did he know? I resisted the urge to pursue this, intent on keeping him on track.

'Two weeks later, the police picked you up.'

'Yeah. I went "no comment" for long enough, but they're talking about me being at the scene and how much easier it'll go if I give them something. They know I'm a user and they've filled in the medical sheet. I need something. If I say yes, they'll fix me up.'

It beggared belief. Preventing this sort of coercion had been at the heart of changes to police procedure. The Police and Criminal Evidence Act laid out clear guidelines for every aspect of criminal investigation. The police deal with drug users a great deal and under PACE rules would be well aware of the danger of obtaining a confession from an addict who was suffering withdrawal symptoms, not least because it would be regarded as unsafe by the Crown Prosecution Service. And that's not what you want in a murder case.

'Did the officers interviewing you actually say that?'

He scowled. 'I don't remember. But they didn't need to: I knew the score.' A whine of defensiveness. So perhaps things hadn't gone down as he was claiming.

'Had you seen a doctor?' I said.

'Custody nurse.' He nodded. So they had followed procedure – he had been given a medical assessment. 'I was using coke and she wouldn't give me anything. I had to see the doctor first and they weren't there till later.'

'But you knew you would see a doctor?' I was still trying to untangle what he was saying – whether he had been coerced or not.

'And you know what he said?' Damien was fired up, sitting up straighter in his chair, chin thrust towards me. 'That they didn't prescribe for cocaine withdrawal. If I'd been a junkie I'd have got a methadone script. But 'cos it's coke they just let you suffer. That is well bad, man.'

There was little to be gained from letting him pick over his outrage at the force's agreed drug abuse policies. So I asked him about later events. 'Your confession – you didn't retract it until after you were imprisoned. You stuck by it at court, when you entered your plea and for sentencing. Why?'

'I didn't think anyone would believe me,' he said quickly. Then he rubbed at his face with his hands and cleared his throat. He averted his gaze. 'I can't do time,' he spoke quietly, 'it's doing my head in.' I suddenly saw a different side to the man: sombre, honest, vulnerable. I wondered whether that was the reason for his volte-face. Not that he was innocent but that it was the only way he could see to get out of jail.

Just as quickly his demeanour switched again: edgy, salacious, a glitter in his eyes. 'There's a ghost, you know, on my wing, B wing, where the condemned cell was. I've seen him. Just before dawn. A man in a dark suit and he's carrying a briefcase. The air goes cold. They say it's John Ellis; he was the hangman, but it drove him mad and he killed himself – slit his own throat.' He gloried in the details.

I took a breath. 'Damien—'

'I've done the short rehab course,' he said, 'but in here.' He shrugged. 'You could come again, bring us something.'

Asking me for drugs! Shock must have registered on my face because he grinned. 'Joke.' That angel smile. 'Some chocolate.'

'Is there anything else you remember? Any other details?'

He shrugged. 'What like?'

Did he expect me to supply them? 'What you've told me is all a bit general, a bit vague,' I said.

'You saying I'm lying?'

'You just don't seem to remember very much.'

'I was in a mess,' he protested, 'and something like that, it shakes you up. I remember the smell.' He shuddered. 'Made me sick, you know. I threw up by the gate.'

'Anything else?'

He shook his head.

'Did you see anyone? Anyone see you?'

Another shake of the head, then he stopped and his eyes brightened. 'There was this guy, coming down the hill when I was going up from the bus. Maybe he done it?'

'Can you describe him?'

A shrug. 'It was dark.'

'Young, old, fat, thin?'

'Dunno,' he said lamely. 'It was freezing, I wasn't hanging about, you know.' He shuffled in his chair. 'You seen that *Most Haunted* on the telly? They want to come in here. Hah! No way they'll get through the night.' He was off again, talking trivia instead of pleading his case.

I gathered together my papers.

'You coming again?'

'I don't know.' I made eye contact.

He looked away, his jaw working, rocking back in his chair. 'You going to talk to my lawyer?'

I looked across; he slid his eyes to meet mine. 'And say what?' I asked him.

I came away feeling even more bemused about Damien Beswick than before I'd met him. His account of events was patchy and paltry. His explanation as to why he'd admitted to the crime was half-baked. I'd no idea what I was going to tell Libby.

SIX

The wind had got up, gusts shaking the trees and pushing banks of slate-grey clouds across the sky. I could smell the peaty aroma of leaf mould amid the petrol fumes and a trace of spice and onion, which made my mouth water, from one of the takeaways on the main road below the prison.

There was still some time before I had to get back home so I paid an unannounced call on Heather Carter, Charlie's widow. I suspected if I rang first I'd get the brush-off. For the family of a victim, the apprehension of the killer is a huge part of dealing with the loss. They know who is responsible at the very least. If the convicted person then starts crying innocence, it's a fresh trauma. Not something any family would want to accept.

Heather and her son Alex still lived on the riverside in Hale by the Bollin. The Carter house stood in its own grounds, bristling with security devices like all the properties nearby. The gates were open, perhaps because it was daylight, but I wondered if the cameras were filming me.

Heather Carter answered the door. I recognized her from the photos in news reports that I'd found online. I introduced myself and asked whether she could spare me a few minutes: I was working on a case linked to her husband's death.

Her eyes narrowed and she took a step back. 'Are you the press?'

'No.' I handed her my business card. 'A private investigator.'

She hesitated. I thought I'd blown it, but then she inclined her head and invited me in.

Heather was short with a mass of curly black hair. She wore trendy glasses, black and red rectangular frames, and was dressed in a cherry-red sweater and fitted chocolate-brown slacks which showed off her curves. She still wore her wedding ring.

The house was lovely: thick carpets and luxurious curtains, high ceilings and huge windows which let in plenty of light. There were several doors off the entrance hall and I guessed there were three or four reception rooms. Heather led me into one which served as a formal dining room. In the centre was a large teak table and chairs, and along one wall a matching sideboard arrayed with family photos.

As we sat down, I heard footfall above and glanced upwards.

'My son, Alex.' Heather smiled. 'Heavy on his feet.'

'How old?'

'Eighteen now.' Her smile faded, her eyes softened. 'He took Charlie's death very hard – I don't know if he'll ever get over it.' She shook her head then adopted a more businesslike tone. 'So, how can I help?'

'I'm reviewing the circumstances around Damien Beswick's conviction.'

Heather frowned.

'Did you receive a letter from his sister, Chloe?'

'Yes,' her face was alert, 'I burnt it. I almost went to the police,' she said. 'The cheek of it!' She gave a brittle laugh. 'Is that who you're working for?' She was riled: circles of anger flared on her cheeks.

'No. I'm sorry, I can't reveal the identity of my client.' Would she guess it was Libby? I thought not. The normal assumption would be that it was someone connected to Damien who'd employ me.

'That man killed my husband. I *know*,' she emphasized the word. 'I've no idea what he or his sister hope to gain from this and I don't give a damn. He's where he should be.' Tears stood in her eyes and I felt a sweep of pity for bringing this to her door.

There were footsteps on the stairs. 'Mum?' a voice called out.

'I'm in here,' she sniffed, taking a breath.

Alex Carter pushed open the door and came in. He stopped short when he saw she had company. He'd inherited his mother's wayward hair and his father's bigger build but he was rangy rather than blocky. He wore black jeans and a plain blue sweatshirt. He avoided eye contact and I formed the impression he was shy and awkward with strangers. 'I'm going now,' he said.

Heather stood up, wishing him good luck as she crossed the room and touched him on the shoulder. 'Just try to relax.'

He nodded, dipped his head and left.

'Driving test,' she told me as she came back to her seat. 'Second time.' She paused, then said: 'Exactly why are you here?'

'I'm trying to establish whether there might be any truth in Damien Beswick's new position. If there is any possibility that they might have got the wrong man.'

Her face hardened and I thought she would sling me out. 'You know what happened?' she demanded.

'I've read about it.'

'Charlie—' The name unseated her this time and I was alarmed to see her mouth quiver and her eyes swim with tears.

'I'm sorry; this is very upsetting for you.'

'It brings it all back,' she said quietly. 'You can't imagine. Charlie never hurt a soul; he was a good man. The shock . . .' She took her glasses off, wiped her eyes, replaced them. Put her hand to her forehead. 'I'd like you to go now.' Suddenly drained.

'Please, Mrs Carter, I won't bother you again but if you could just tell me what you remember.' I was pushing it; the woman was in bits and I was asking her to rake it all up. 'Please? And then I'll leave you alone.'

She looked directly at me. Her mouth was taut and trembling.

'We didn't part on good terms. That still makes me so sad. You probably read that Charlie was seeing someone else?'

I nodded.

'He'd told me he wouldn't see her for a while. It was a chance for us to give it another go, see if we could make it work.'

In Heather's eyes. But from Libby's point of view the marriage was past saving; it was simply a compassionate pause in Charlie's new relationship for the sake of the boy.

'That Saturday Charlie said he was going to a sales exhibition at the NEC in Birmingham.' She ducked her head, studying her hands. 'I didn't believe him.' She looked up, stretching her neck, rubbing one hand up and down it then covering her mouth and giving a shaky sigh. Her anguish was palpable but I waited quietly for her to continue.

'I got a friend to come round and I'm not proud of this now . . .' her brow furrowed and she sniffed hard '. . . but we followed him in her car. As soon as he turned off for Thornsby instead of staying on the road to the M6, I knew he'd lied to me. He was sneaking off to see her.' Tears coursed down her cheeks and she swept them away. 'Sorry.'

'No,' I murmured, feeling lousy.

'So we turned round and drove back here. I was calling him all the names under the sun but he was—' She didn't complete the sentence but I knew what she was saying: he was dead or dying. 'That made it even worse. That those were my last memories of him.'

'I'm sorry. There weren't any other suspects?' I asked her.

She looked a bit muddled – still lost in the past, her nose red and puffy from crying. 'No. Well, the girlfriend.' I noticed she avoided Libby's name. 'Then they found Damien Beswick. If Charlie had just given him his wallet, instead of trying to hang on to it, then he might still be here.' She went and fetched a tissue from a box on the sideboard, blew her nose. In Damien's new version of events the wallet was on the kitchen counter; in his original confession the knife had been beside it.

'Maybe we would have gone our separate ways,' Heather said, 'but Alex would still have his father.'

And so would Libby's daughter. Had Heather known that Libby was pregnant? It hadn't been in the papers. The women had no contact so I could only assume that Heather had no inkling of Rowena's existence. I imagined it would be even harder if she had done. To discover that Charlie had been on the brink of starting a new family when he died, replicating what Heather and Alex had shared with him, would have been an extra grief.

She fell quiet.

After a moment or two, she asked: 'He couldn't get a retrial, could he?'

'He'd have to present new evidence.'

She nodded, reassured.

We made small talk as she showed me out. The house was warm but she shivered and rubbed at her arms, the chill of murder in the air.

I had parked on the roadside. Above the high wall, tall shrubs and specimen trees seethed in the wind. I could see some sort of palm and a lovely graceful fir, the spiral of its branches reminiscent of Japanese watercolour paintings. My phone rang before I could start the car. It was Chloe Beswick. 'Did you see him?'

'Yes.'

'And?'

'Chloe, I'm not sure what you expect me to say.' I sighed.

'You believe him – that'd be a good start,' she said baldly.

'I'm not sure I do. He wasn't very coherent; he kept going off at a tangent. He didn't say anything that would count as new evidence. Frankly he seemed to be evading my questions.'

She swore. 'Wanker! I told him. So, you just giving up, are you? 'Cos I'm not.' I couldn't help but admire her determination. She'd a losing hand with Damien to defend but she was with him all the way.

'I'm working for Libby Hill,' I reminded her, 'not you.'

'You're not totally sure about it, though, are you? If you could just talk to him some more—'

'I don't know yet. Let me think about it, see some more people.'

'OK.' She sounded disappointed.

'Oh, he wants you to take him some tobacco,' I said.

'I always do, cheeky git.'

*   *   *

Had Damien Beswick killed Charlie Carter or had he made a false confession? I spent the next hour in my office, researching the phenomena. Most articles stressed that the area was complex and several factors were involved when someone made a false confession. There were three broad categories: voluntary confessions, compliant false confessions and internalized false confessions. I reckoned I could rule out the first – Damien had not walked into a police station claiming responsibility for the murder. He hadn't been seeking fame and notoriety or meaning for his life as most of these people did. His confession was only made once he'd been arrested and in the middle of interviews. There were elements in both the other categories that I thought might fit with Damien Beswick. Compliant false confessions are made by those who see no other way out. The suspect thinks if he confesses he will get away, get help, be allowed to leave. Damien had been panicking about his drug supply being cut off. He hoped to see the doctor; he hoped the doctor would give him something to manage the withdrawal symptoms he was experiencing. On the other hand, he also fit the picture of an internalized false confession: people who are highly suggestible and over the course of questioning come to believe they may be guilty.

Damien Beswick was suggestible. He had been at the scene, his memory of events was fragmented, he was eager to finish the questions and end the interview to get drugs. The fact that his memory of events was so poor was a major obstacle to establishing if he was lying now – or had been lying when he owned up.

The friend that Heather had enlisted to trail her cheating husband, the one Libby had told me about, was Valerie Mayhew, a retired teacher and a justice of the peace. Mayhew is not a common name in Manchester and it was easy enough to find her in the phone book. She answered my call on her way out to a meeting at the Civil Justice Centre. She would have put me off but I asked whether she could spare me ten minutes over a coffee if I came into town, telling her it related to the Charlie Carter case. She relented; I think her interest was piqued.

The Civil Justice Centre is a brave new building in the Spinningfields area of the city centre. It's an audacious design:

a tall, thin central skyscraper with glassy boxes jutting out irregu-
larly at either end; coloured battleship grey and primrose yellow,
it looks a bit like a Jenga toy tower made of snazzy shipping
containers, defying gravity with their overhangs. The feel as you
enter is of a sweeping space, a hotel or conference centre, perhaps.
The atrium soars twenty stories high and each floor has vistas
to the Pennine hills that fringe the city to the north and the east.
A bank of lifts whisk people heavenward to their fates: for adop-
tion, bankruptcy, custody hearings. There's a café on the ground
floor where Valerie had arranged to see me. I had described
myself (grey wool pea-coat, turquoise scarf) and she waved me
over. A woman in a navy trouser suit with silver-grey shoulder-
length hair, expertly cut. Valerie had fantastic bone structure so,
although her face was heavily lined with age, she was still very
attractive. She'd paid attention to her teeth, too: they gleamed
white and regular.

Valerie had finished a snack and I refused her offer of a drink
and sat across the table from her.

'You went to see Heather?' she asked. 'How was she?'

'Upset.'

'It's still very raw,' she said. 'You don't put any store by
Damien Beswick's retraction?' There was a no-nonsense, teacher-
ish tone in her voice which got my back up.

'I'm keeping an open mind,' I said, 'still building up a picture
of events. That's why I wanted to talk to you.'

She weighed me up for a moment. 'OK,' inviting me to proceed.

'Just describe that day,' I said.

'Heather rang me in a complete state, mid-afternoon. Charlie
had told her he was off to some sales convention in Birmingham
but she didn't believe him. He'd more than enough work on and
he'd never touted for jobs outside the north-west before. She
thought he was using it as an excuse to go see this other woman.'

'Libby Hill?'

Valerie nodded.

'Heather had already told you about her?' I asked.

'Yes. He'd agreed to stop seeing this woman for a few months.
They didn't want to mess up Alex's exams and I think Heather
hoped he would come to his senses. But then she suspected he'd
broken his promise and asked me to help her find out one way or

the other. She thought if we used my car Charlie wouldn't notice.' Valerie shrugged and rearranged her plate on the tray in front of her. 'It all seemed a bit . . . seedy.' She looked up. 'I suppose it's the sort of thing you do all the time, in your line,' she said dryly.

'Oh, yes,' I agreed.

'So, I tried to dissuade her but she was set on catching him out and I owed Heather a lot. She'd been brilliant when my own marriage was breaking up.' She shrugged. 'I couldn't say no.'

'How did you know each other?'

'Through church.' Valerie caught sight of someone across the foyer and waved hello. She turned back to me. 'I went round there, called for Heather and we parked a few hundred yards down the main road. When Charlie came out and turned right at the junction, we would go after him. We didn't have long to wait. He set off about four.' She frowned. 'It really was the most horrible, awful irony.' She gave her head a little shake. 'As you probably heard from Heather, we followed him until the turning for Thornsby and off he sailed. The opposite route from Birmingham. Heather knew he must be going up to the cottage. She was furious – hurt, too. We went back to hers and I didn't feel I could leave her like that so I stayed with her. Alex was there but he didn't know about any of it.'

'Didn't he realize something was going on?'

'No, he was in his room most of the time. Meant to be cramming in revision for his mocks but it sounded like he'd got some video game playing. We do advise them to revise to music but not that sort of racket.' She was being sardonic. 'Heather had to tell him to turn it down. He came downstairs for tea but she let him take it up to eat, so I doubt he noticed the state she was in. Then, at seven, the police came.' She shook her head slowly. 'Devastating,' she said simply.

A waitress began clearing the table. Valerie checked her watch.

'And when you heard they'd charged Damien Beswick?'

'Relief.'

'You never had any doubts?'

'Good grief, no. He owned up, the evidence fit. Kids like that: dysfunctional family, drugs, crime – sooner or later there's violence.' She pushed back her chair. 'We see it all the time.'

*   *   *

The wind had brought rain with it – not heavy yet, just squalls that spat drops at me. As I walked back through the complex in the direction of the car I felt dwarfed by the buildings lowering over me and a little overwhelmed by the investigation. It wasn't the complexity of it; after all, it boiled down to one question: was Damien Beswick lying then, or now? But it was the frustration of not being able to tell whether he was guilty or wrongly convicted and the sense that there was no easy path I could follow to clearly establish that. Before his conviction the emphasis had been on proving Damien culpable beyond any reasonable doubt; now the reverse was true. In the balance of probability he had killed Charlie – it would need some stunning evidence to convince anyone otherwise.

Ray had left me a text: *clothes – no joy*. So I called into Children's World on my way home. It stocked every possible accessory and accoutrement. I found myself drooling over patterned towelling Babygros and funky baby sweaters, instead of just grabbing the two-for-a-tenner value packs in the dump bins. I could have spent a fortune and stayed all day but I got a grip, reminded myself that Jamie might be gone by teatime and settled on three cheapish cotton all-in-ones in powder blue, dusky rose and white with stars and moons.

The place didn't sell small sets of nappies; the ones they had would need a forklift truck to shift them. But there was a special offer on starter packs of three reusables. They'd a terry towelling inside and a plastic outer coating, fitted with velcro tabs. I'd used something similar for Maddie when I'd read how it took hundreds of years for disposables to degrade in landfill.

As I negotiated the traffic home, I mused on how the world seemed full of babies: Jamie, Chloe's little one, Libby's daughter. How old was Rowena? Due in June, Libby had said, so she'd be three months or so. The possibility stuck in my mind like a fishbone in the throat. I couldn't dislodge it. With it came a creeping unease, a quickening of my pulse. Why hadn't it occurred to me before? Because it seemed so unlikely – that a new client would dump her child on me? It was unlikely *whoever* had done it. It was ridiculous – still I had to ring her, had to know.

Parking in our drive, I pulled out my phone and found her

number. I would get myself invited there to give her feedback
– explain I understood it would be harder for her to come to me
with a baby in tow. If she tried to wriggle out of it, then I'd
know I was on to something. Maybe I'd have to ask her outright.
My throat felt dry as I entered her number.

Libby answered the phone and I heard the deafening cries of
a howling baby close by. Relief rippled through me like a drug.
'Libby, Sal Kilkenny.'

'Hi.'

'Not a good time? I just wanted to fix up a meeting. Are you
free tomorrow?'

'I can do mid-morning, say, half ten.' The crying became even
more frantic. 'Sorry, I'll have to go,' she added.

'See you tomorrow.'

It was quiet in my house. I peeked in the lounge and found Jamie,
wrapped in a blanket, asleep on the sofa. Ray was in the kitchen,
reading the paper after his lunch. I was five minutes later than
I'd said. Would I get a lecture?

'Hi,' I greeted him. 'I got some clothes. Has she been OK?'

'Not bad. Just gone off.'

'You going into work?'

He paused. I looked at him. Was there something wrong? My
stomach constricted. He shifted the chair, got to his feet. Then
I saw it: the invitation stark in his eyes, the way his lips parted
slightly, the rise of his chest.

I walked to meet him. Felt his hands in my hair, the brush of
his moustache, then his lips on mine and his tongue, firm and
smooth and warm. There was a sizzling sensation in my breasts
and belly, the flush of heat between my thighs. I pulled away,
hungry, breathless, savouring the intensity of his gaze. Those
rich, brown eyes.

'Your bed or mine,' I whispered.

He grabbed my waist, pulled me close, then raised his hand
to the top button on my shirt. 'Who said anything about bed?'

With huge consideration Jamie slept for two and a half hours
and was still asleep when it was time to fetch Maddie and Tom.
So was Ray. We'd decamped to my room for a post-coital rest

and now he was lying on his back, snoring lightly, his long lashes casting shadows on his cheeks, the curls at the edge of his temples damp with perspiration.

I showered quickly and dressed, scooped up the baby and put her in the buggy, lowered the rain hood and set off.

The rain battered down, drumming on the plastic cover of the buggy, bouncing off the flagstones. The air was fresh, strong with the dark, watery smell of wet stone. I barrelled along, almost enjoying the weather. Still high from love-making, still smitten by the man who I had never imagined I'd fall in love with. And relieved that I had been able to forget, for a couple of delicious hours, that I was no closer to solving the mystery of who had left a foundling on my doorstep.

SEVEN

Jamie shared my bath that evening. I could have washed her in the sink or top and tailed her; after all I'd already showered so I didn't need a soak, but there's nothing quite so pleasant and calming as bathing with a baby.

It had been my escape route when I had Maddie. As a single parent, there was no one close by to help me look after her. We had some hard times: days when she'd run me ragged and I'd be in tears at the sheer scale of it all. The lack of sleep, the fact that it took so long to change her, to feed her, that there was never any respite.

When I reached fever pitch, or she did, there was the fail-safe option of the bath. My gas bills soared but it was worth every penny. Afternoons would often find us submerged together. When she was particularly fractious we might end up having two baths in one day. I'd run the water, walking to and fro with her as she cried. Her protests accelerated when I undressed her: her face contorted, red with fury, limbs rigid, her cries so sharp they made my breasts leak milk. Then I would pull off my own clothes, lift her up, climb into the water and lower her in, brace her on my knees so she could see me. As the water lapped at her feet, then her bottom and up to her chest, her cries would falter, shrivel to gusty breaths then fade. The magic of water: a return to the womb.

I was ready for bed by nine thirty and didn't resist. Jamie had me up at midnight, three a.m. and five thirty. Consequently by the time Libby Hill arrived for our meeting the next morning I felt like death warmed up.

I'd rung Abi Dobson the previous evening and lined her up to look after Jamie while I saw my client. I spun her the same story about Jamie being a friend's child I was looking after while she had an operation. Abi was delighted. 'More practise,' she said. 'I'm doing loads of childcare at the moment.'

'You ought to make the most of the time you've got left,' I warned her.

'Everyone says that.'

'Yeah, because we all wish we had. You won't have time to wipe your nose once the baby comes.'

Abi looked amazing when she opened the door to us. She was tanned and her hair streaked from travelling in Thailand and India, and she wore some stretchy knit combination that hugged her huge belly.

'How are you feeling?' I asked her. 'You look great.'

'I'm good.' She lifted Jamie out of the buggy. 'Apart from the piles.'

I groaned in sympathy.

When Libby arrived, I outlined for her what I'd done so far and was honest with her about my uncertainty.

'So, you're saying you can't tell one way or the other?' she asked me, her grey eyes piercing.

'If you pushed me, I'd say he's more likely to be guilty than not. But if you take away the confession, I've no idea how strong the other evidence is. Partly because I don't know exactly what they've got. We all know he was at the cottage, that he stole Charlie's wallet and that there was blood on his footwear – but how secure is the forensic evidence that he used the knife? I'd have to be in the police to get that sort of information. They never found the weapon, did they? So it will be impossible to prove Damien used it, I think.'

Libby sighed, irritated by the unsatisfactory nature of my report. 'So that's it. Well, what else could you do?'

'Try and see Damien's lawyer, perhaps. They would know what evidence the CPS had. Though Chloe Beswick says they told her loud and clear that there are no grounds for an appeal. She's asked me to talk to Damien again. It's up to you,' I told her. 'You don't need to decide now. He's not going anywhere. Do you want to think about it?'

'Yeah,' she said. Then she thought of something, leant forward with her hands on her knees. 'What if you could talk to someone in the police?'

'That would help. Why?'

'It's just – there was one of the detectives; he questioned me when I was a suspect.' She gave a bitter laugh, still hurt at the treatment she received. 'But after that he kept in touch, let me know where they were up to. He informed me when they arrested Damien Beswick and he told me when they had a confession. It was good of him. I didn't have a family liaison officer as such but he did it anyway. He might see you.'

'What's he called?'

'Geoff Sinclair – he's based at Longsight. I did try him when the letter came, but he was off work.'

'I'll try that, then?' I said.

'Yes.' She seemed happier at the prospect than she had at me giving up. She wanted to get to the bottom of things and not be left with any doubts or ambiguity.

After she'd left I rang Greater Manchester Police and asked to be put through to Longsight; I was passed around a bit and was finally told that Detective Sinclair had retired.

When I rang Libby, she was disappointed but asked me if I could try and contact him anyway. She knew he lived in New Mills, a village up in the peaks beyond Stockport.

Luckily Sinclair had a BT phone line. That meant he was in the directory. With the plethora of telecoms providers, many subscribers are no longer listed. It isn't impossible to find people on other networks – it just takes longer.

He was home. He listened to my spiel about working on behalf of Libby Hill (I was sure that using her name would get me further than leaving it out) and I told him that both Libby and

Heather Carter had received letters claiming Damien Beswick was innocent.

'Tell her to chuck it in the bin,' he said, in a blunt Lancashire accent.

'She won't do that, not yet anyway. Can I come and see you?'

'Why?' He was guarded.

'Libby wants to be certain that the conviction was sound. If I knew some of the police evidence that supported his confession—'

'I don't know,' he said.

'I could be there by one,' I pressed on. 'It's been a terrible shock for her and she really appreciated how you kept her informed during the enquiry. You could help me set her mind at ease.' What's a little emotional blackmail between investigators?

'I'll need to be done by two,' he said flatly. 'And you'll have to park in the pub car park on Crown Street.'

Result!

I left Jamie in Abi's care and made the trip out along the A6 through the suburbs beyond Stockport. The road narrows frequently and is choked with traffic. It got easier once I forked left and climbed up past Lyme Park, scene of the famous white shirt fandango with Mr Darcy in a television adaptation of *Pride and Prejudice*. If you didn't see it think hunk with smouldering eyes and a manly chest drenched in wet white cotton. On through Disley and from there the road clung to the hillside as the valleys opened out and the peaks came into view. New Mills is famous for its textile mills and sweet factory (Swizzles, home to Refreshers, Love Hearts and Drumstick lollies) and, more recently, renowned for the innovative hydroelectricity scheme sited on an old weir.

Geoff Sinclair looked like Gollum from *The Lord of the Rings* movies – well, a middle-aged version. Bald-headed with wide cheekbones, big ears and a long, scrawny neck, bulbous startling blue eyes and rubberiness to his lips. Large hands with spidery fingers. Unlike the ghostly creature in the films, his complexion was sallow, yellow. It was hard to tell his age: his face was wrinkled but I'd have guessed fifties rather than sixties. Police can retire after twenty-five or thirty years on a pension, so if he had joined up as a young man he may only have been fifty or so now.

We didn't shake hands but he invited me in with a nod of the head. His cottage was on the outskirts of town and the living room had a broad window running across the main wall at the back, facing out on to the hills and the valley below. Nature in wide-screen. It was another breezy day and a stand of hawthorns to the left of Sinclair's garden, bent low to the hill, shivered in the wind.

'Would you like a brew?' he offered. 'There's a pot just made.'

I thanked him and he disappeared into the kitchen while I sat and drank in the view. As the hills rose from the valley floor, I could see where farmland gave way to the moors, the green and tawny pastures replaced by dark splashes of peat bog, swathes of purple heather and orange-coloured bracken. I made out the hulk of Kinder Scout, the area's highest peak: a gritstone plateau, a sometimes wild and treacherous place to walk. Clouds like boulders, dense and rounded, swept over the mountain. It'd be a punishing commute to work in Manchester from here but maybe the trade-off was worth it.

The tea came, hot and strong, bitter on the tongue. Just the way I like it. Aware that my time was limited, I began by showing him Chloe's letter. He read it and snorted, a plosive 'pah' from his lips.

'I went to see her, then I visited Damien,' I told him.

'He still in Strangeways?'

I nodded.

'So, what's his story?' he sounded deeply suspicious as he lifted his mug.

'Garbled, to say the least. He says Charlie was already dead when he entered the cottage. He claims he confessed because he was suffering from withdrawal symptoms and it was the easiest way to end the interview and get some medical attention.'

'He entered a guilty plea,' Sinclair said deliberately. He blew on his tea and took a sip.

'Yes,' I agreed, 'but then he told his sister he'd made it up.'

'He's mucking you about,' he said.

'Maybe. But if you set aside the confession and his presence at the scene, what other evidence did you have? You didn't have the weapon.'

'Never found.' He pulled a face. 'Beswick said he'd chucked it away – wouldn't or couldn't say where.'

'Was it his knife?'

'No. He said it was at the cottage, on the work surface. When Charlie came at him, Beswick grabbed it. One stab wound to the stomach. But Beswick's narrative of events matched everything at the scene. Everything,' he repeated, locking those large eyes on mine. 'There were no loose ends, no discrepancies. He's wasting your time.'

Personally I thought the absence of the murder weapon was rather a loose end but I didn't want to aggravate him. I wasn't going to just drop it, though. 'Did you interview him?' I asked.

'No.' He took another sip of his tea.

I was disappointed, thinking he wouldn't have as much information if he hadn't heard it first-hand. 'But Damien was at the cottage,' I pointed out. 'He'd have picked up details from being there, wouldn't he, even if he hadn't been the one to attack Charlie? Like where the body was and the fact that Charlie had been stabbed?'

Sinclair's eyes, wide and glassy, like blue mints, bore into me. 'It's possible,' he allowed. His long fingers curled round his mug.

'How much detail did he give?' I asked. 'He could barely remember anything when I asked him to talk me through it,' I said. 'Surely the police would expect it to be coherent and detailed.'

'He'd taken drugs that day, on the way to the cottage – did he tell you that?'

Annoyance flickered inside me; Sinclair noticed and gave a little nod. If Damien had been doped up, it could well affect his recollection of events.

'What you're not taking into account,' Sinclair said, 'is that the detectives talking to him would have been trained in advanced interview techniques. You have a suspect who says they can't remember and there are ways and means to access those memories.'

'Like what?' I was interested professionally, although a major difference between my role and that of the police when talking to people is that I have no authority. The people I speak to can clam up, get up and walk away, refuse to let me over the threshold. I can't 'detain' anyone for questioning.

Sinclair set down the cup and winced: an irritable, grumpy

old man not wanting to explain. Nevertheless, he began to answer my question, his hands gesturing expressively as he spoke. His wrists were bony, jutting from his pullover, and I wondered if he lived alone, and if he'd let mealtimes slide in the weeks since he'd retired.

'Take a mugging,' he began. 'It's all a blur to the victim – didn't get a good look at the mugger and so on. But they do mention it had just started raining. Well, we take that one concrete detail and build on it: what sounds were there when it started raining? Was it cold or warm? Had anyone just passed them? Do they remember what colour coat the person was wearing?'

'Appealing to the senses?' I saw what he meant.

'That's what memories are made of.'

Like a smell bringing back a particular time in life, or a piece of music triggering a memory. I thought about it. There had been precious few sense memories in Damien's story when I spoke to him: 'it was freezing' was one, the smell in the cottage another.

'I wasn't in on those interviews,' Sinclair said. 'Beswick's recollection was hazy at times because of the drugs, but it still fit the known facts. Fit like a glove. Now, if his new version is a load of tripe, then keeping it vague, ill-defined and sketchy is safer for him. If you're lying you keep it simple, say the minimum, so there's less to trip you up. Telling the truth you can elaborate, illustrate your story, you don't need to worry about contradicting yourself. The memories are solid. The details are there.'

I looked out to the hills while I considered what he'd said. A fierce gust of wind rattled the hawthorn and a crow landed on the dry stone wall at the bottom of the garden, its plumage dark and ragged.

'One thing he did say was that the door was unlocked. Why would Charlie not lock up?' I said.

'Maybe he was coming in and out, fetching things from the car. And he was expecting Libby, remember.'

'But the lights were off: that's what drew Damien to the cottage,' I said. 'He thought it was empty.'

Sinclair shook his head. 'It's more likely he turned them off after.'

'Why?'

'It's a natural impulse, to conceal a crime. The criminal will want to hide the body, delay detection, obscure the truth.'

'Damien said he was sick by the gate.' Another clear detail – was it a lie?

'That's right,' Sinclair confirmed.

'And he saw a man walking down the hill,' I said.

Sinclair frowned, creases rippling across his wide brow. 'First I've heard of it.'

'Someone coming down the hill as Damien was going up from the bus,' I said.

'We'd nothing like that on house-to-house. There was no mention of that,' he said. 'We hadn't any witnesses in the vicinity, not a soul.' Sinclair closed his eyes for a moment. I waited. 'Did Beswick imply that this man might be the real killer?' he asked, sarcasm ripe in his tone.

'Yes,' I admitted.

He gave a snort. 'There you go, then. He knows we have no other suspects so he conjures someone out of thin air.'

Was that the case? Damien inventing a bogeyman in the dark – a shadowy figure who'd never come forward? Something, someone to give his retraction more credence.

'Why was Libby a suspect?' I asked him.

'She found the body, she'd been at the scene, she had a close relationship to the deceased. We had to eliminate her. Standard practice.'

'But what motive would she have?' Above the slopes of Kinder, a bird was cruising on a slipstream.

'Lover's tiff. He tells her he's going back to the wife and she loses it. Or she tells him about the baby and he wants to send her packing.' He paused. 'She had the baby all right?'

'Yes, a girl.'

He dipped his chin, satisfied. 'It's always a sensitive area.' He went on: 'Those close to the victim are key candidates for the crime. No one likes putting a person who has just lost a loved one through a bout of questioning, and it is done with great sensitivity, but it has to be done.'

'And you never had any doubts that you got the right man?'

'None,' he said simply.

There was a knock at the door and I got to my feet as Sinclair did. 'Thank you. If I think of anything else, can I ring you?'

He paused, then: 'Yes.'

At the door there was a nurse; she bore a lapel badge with her name on and the logo Macmillan Cancer Support. She smiled then looked past me to Sinclair. 'Good afternoon, Geoff.'

I said goodbye. She stood aside to let me pass, then went in.

A host of tiny clues fell into place: the man's jaundiced colour, his lack of hair or eyebrows, his skeletal frame, his 'retirement', the way he'd winced at one point as he set his cup down. Geoff Sinclair was battling cancer.

Why had he agreed to see me? I felt slightly guilty that I'd pushed to meet him: surely a sick person had other priorities. But then I talked myself round: wasn't I just being patronizing? Sick or not, Geoff Sinclair was a grown-up, more than capable of deciding for himself whether to respond to my request. Perhaps it was it a welcome distraction from his enforced rest. Or maybe he felt obliged, on Libby's account. Whichever, for me there had been progress, not much I grant you, but enough to feel I could usefully take things further.

EIGHT

I picked up Jamie and paid Abi for her time. Although I had chores to do, I could take the baby with me.

Pushing her up the road to the centre of Withington, near where we live, I enjoyed the walk. The wind and rain had ebbed away, taking the clouds too and leaving a high blue sky where gulls wheeled and cried. The sun, its light suffused, warm and golden, made the colour of the leaves sing bronze and crimson, copper and nut brown. In the sycamores by the fire station, starlings thronged the branches, yattering at each other. Someone had been cutting back conifers in the graveyard by the church and the crisp scent of pine sap bit the air.

They'd pulled the old cinema down. Cine City. The iconic building, originally called The Scala, had been the third picture house to open in the whole of the country but it had fallen into neglect, failing to compete with the multiplexes and all attempts to save it had floundered. Now there was a gaping hole. Ongoing wrangles between the developer and the city planners had delayed the start of building work. I'd seen some of the designs in the *South Manchester Reporter*, our local free sheet – apartments above shopping units: glass, wood and steel, like a thousand other buildings in a thousand other towns. It made me want to weep. The White Lion pub, with its distinctive round clock tower, stood alongside the gap at the junction of the main roads and marked the southernmost end of the high street. The pub was boarded up, too. Would that be next?

Along the high street some work had been done to improve the area, creating wider pavements and parking bays, but there was no disguising the fact that Withington was a struggling centre. The stretch of shops was punctuated by empty units bristling with To Let and For Sale signs. The businesses that survived were a mix of discount outlets, low-cost hair and beauty salons, newsagents and the odd gem, like the vegetarian café and the chemist. The health food shop had gone, succumbing after years. It was where I had spent much of my hard-earned cash on tofu and lentils and the like. One sector was thriving: rental agencies. There were tons of them, set up to find accommodation for students and young professionals. Match single people with the plethora of flats and apartments built in the boom years. Would they find takers for the ones that would be built on the old cinema site?

When we reached the far end of the shops, I wheeled the buggy up the ramp into the library. My books were overdue and I'd gathered together two of Maddie's that had been mislaid.

The assistant took the pile of books and noticed Jamie in the buggy. 'Congratulations.' She beamed. I was a regular in the library so she knew me by sight. 'I'd no idea. How old?'

'No,' I rushed to correct her, 'not mine. A friend's.'

She laughed, scanned my books on the machine. 'Sorry. Does it make you broody?'

'Maybe a bit,' I admitted, 'but I don't know if I could start that all over again.'

'My eldest is expecting his first,' she confided. 'I'm going to be a grandma.' She gave a little shiver of delight. 'That'll be one pound twenty.'

I congratulated her and fished for change.

'Can't wait.' She returned to her theme. 'And best of all I'll be able to hand the baby back at the end of the day!'

Her question stuck with me as I walked home. Was I broody? Was having another child a possibility? It hadn't really been an issue before; Maddie filled all my maternal cravings – and then some. And I'd not been in any relationships that grew serious enough to think about having a baby.

Ray and I were different: still new enough to be unsettling, exciting, consuming, but based on several years of living together, on friendship and looking after our children together.

When I'd first slept with him, I'd no idea where it would lead. Fearful of jeopardizing what we already shared I had tried to resist the attraction that had sprung up between us. He had made a pass, I'd stalled; he'd wooed me, and teased me, sulked, waited, wooed me some more. My best friend Diane finally told me to go ahead and sleep with him and get it over with, scratch the itch. Reckless – more her style than mine. But I did.

Oh, boy.

The weeks had become months, the sky had not fallen. So what was next? Did there have to be a 'next'? Would he be interested in fatherhood again? He was a great dad. The idea made my stomach flip, like driving over a bump in the road. The idea lodged there then, tickling at the back of my mind. Something daring, almost forbidden. Something to sneak out later and puzzle over.

We passed Christie's, the big cancer hospital. Always busy with staff and visitors, patients and builders, the latter involved in a seemingly endless programme of expansion. It wasn't unusual to see people strolling up this bit of the road clad in pyjamas and pushing a drip, soaking up the precious chance of fresh air and a change of scene. And there were always a bunch of people having that fag before going back in through the glass entrance doors.

Jamie woke; she gave a little crow and screwed up her nose.

I chatted to her and she watched my lips, scrutinized my face with great solemnity. Where was her mother now? Missing her, surely. Tonight would be the third night apart. My theory about the number of nappies equalling the duration of her absence had bitten the dust. When would she be back? Was she there now, at my place waiting for us, full of gratitude and compelling explanations? What if she never came back? My throat tightened at the thought. What then? How long before I'd have to tell someone about Jamie? See her removed into the care of social services? They'd never let her stay with us. We hadn't been vetted or approved. Would we even want her to? A foundling without any history; a child with no biological connection to either of us. Could I love her? Love her like I loved Maddie? And Ray, could he? How long? Ray had asked the same question. A week? Three?

As if catching the souring of my mood, Jamie started to fret.

'Soon home,' I told her, 'and then we'll give you a nice feed.'

Chloe Beswick rang me that evening. She had spoken to her brother and still wanted me to visit him again. Had I thought about it?

'I only saw him yesterday,' I objected.

'I know. But I told him you needed more details and he says he remembered something else. Said he's been racking brains all night and it came back to him.'

This, I doubted. It sounded like a ruse to get me back inside. Why? To brighten his stay, break up the routine? Chloe's belief in Damien's innocence seemed genuine but Damien's belief in himself . . . I still hadn't got the measure of it. Would another visit make things clearer? Hard to tell. Now that I'd spoken to Geoff Sinclair not only did I have more understanding of the forensic evidence but I'd also picked up some tips on advanced interviewing techniques. It would be interesting to try them out.

'OK,' I agreed. 'I'll ring the prison tomorrow—'

'I've booked you in,' she said, quick as a flash. 'Ten o'clock.'

'Really?' I was disconcerted. Suddenly Chloe was arranging my work diary?

'It can be a right pain getting appointments,' she said

unapologetically. 'Thought I'd save you the hassle. If ten's no good—'

'It's fine,' I said, though I still felt railroaded.

'I've warned him – whatever you want to know, he tells you. And if you tell him to shut up he does that an' all – no messing, innit.'

'Chloe, can I ask you something?'

'Free country.'

'Why couldn't he have been more cooperative yesterday if he's serious about making an appeal?'

She sighed. 'It's how he is: brain like a frog, all over the place. The drugs don't help.'

'He's on medication?'

'Stuff to calm him down – makes it hard to concentrate.' Christ, I thought, if that was calm, I'd hate to see him agitated. And he'd talked to me as though he'd no medical help at all.

She carried on: 'Plus whatever else he can get his hands on.' She was nothing if not honest. 'There's more drugs in there than there is out here,' she said. 'So, you're all right for tomorrow?'

'Yes. I'll let you know how I get on.'

Abi Dobson was sorry but she couldn't take Jamie the next morning – she had an antenatal appointment. I couldn't ask Ray; he wouldn't take more time off work to help me out. His mother, Nana Tello, used to stand in sometimes when the kids were smaller as long as it didn't impinge on her other plans. She used to hum and haw and show such reluctance that it got so I disliked asking her. She would not be in the market for babysitting a strange child.

Taking my life in my hands, I rang my friend Diane. Diane is not child friendly. Even though we are very close she has rarely looked after Maddie, though Diane's more relaxed in her company as Maddie gets older. Diane hasn't any kids herself and has no desire to have any. She falls into sexual relationships every so often. Fall being the operative word. She plummets like a rock. Diane's liaisons are a bit like elephant traps: rare, unexpected, dangerous, difficult to get out of. Aside from them her real passion is her work – she's an artist.

I thought of Geoff Sinclair as I waited for her to answer the phone. Like him, Diane had fought cancer. Breast cancer. She'd had a lumpectomy and chemo. They thought they'd got it all. She takes pills every day.

'Hello?'

'Diane, I need to ask you a huge favour.'

'Oh, God,' she groaned.

After the kids were in bed Ray came into the living room where I was feeding Jamie. I smiled across at him but his face remained impassive. He sat down on the armchair. Perched on the edge; ready to strike. I concentrated on the baby and studied her eyes. Felt her feet pedal in time to her sucking. I'd one hand supporting her and the other holding the bottle; not enough hands free to rub her feet, which I used to do when I was breastfeeding Maddie. Ray took an audible breath. I waited.

'Still no word,' he said. 'This is the third night.'

'Yes, I know.' And I wasn't looking forward to yet more fragmented sleep.

'Don't you think you should consider contacting the authorities?'

'No.' I stared across at him, my face warm. 'Not yet.'

'When?'

'Ray, I said before, I'm not setting a deadline.'

'I think you should,' His face was tight; I could feel his disapproval, palpable in every cell of his body.

'You've made that clear.'

'So what, the situation just rolls on and on?'

'It's only been a couple of days,' my voice rose. The baby stiffened. I spoke more quietly, tried to relax my body, fighting against the tension. 'She's happy, she's safe.'

'She's not yours.'

'I know that!' I glared at him. He was talking to me like I was some deranged woman living in a fantasy. 'And I'll be more than happy to see her mother show up. Meanwhile, I'll carry on looking after her as best as I can.' I lost the struggle to keep calm; my voice shook, my heart was thundering in my chest. I wanted to throw something at him. Jamie had stopped sucking.

He watched me for a moment, then looked away exasperated, his jaw muscle tautening. He turned back, about to speak, I thought, but then he got to his feet and walked out. I called after him but he didn't return.

There was no pattern to the nights. Jamie was still awake at ten so I fed her then. She slept through until half three. Five hours. I could have had five hours unbroken kip if I'd gone to sleep myself but I probably wasted two hours tossing and turning, feeling anxious about Ray, about the baby.

The tension remained with me the following day, aggravated by tiredness. My shoulder was stiff and my neck ached. There was a knot of worry in my stomach.

Maddie got into a panic at breakfast – she couldn't find her PE kit. Jamie was bawling and I was hurriedly mixing a feed.

Tom put his hands over his ears. 'Shut up, shut up, shut up,' he chanted.

'It's not in my drawers,' Maddie insisted, 'you look.'

'Try the cellar,' I said. 'It might be in the dryer.'

Her face fell.

'For heaven's sake, Maddie,' I snapped. 'It's broad daylight, there's a window down there and you can put the light on too if you need.' The dark is one of Maddie's fears.

The baby cried louder. 'I can't go,' I explained. 'I need to feed Jamie.'

'Ray can feed her,' Maddie whined.

Ray slid a look my way, mutinous, critical but nevertheless moved closer and held his hands out for Jamie. She was in full throttle, face tomato red, back arching with frustration, twisting her head this way and that. Her cries were agonizing to hear. You are more at risk of being killed in the first twelve months of life than at any other time. It was a fact I could understand, horrible though that sounds. We arrive in the world completely vulnerable, utterly dependent on others and furnished with vocal chords that shred a listener's nerves to bits.

When I opened the cellar door, Digger emerged, gave a foolish little woof and wove about my legs, wagging his tail.

'Digger's here,' I called out to Ray who looked after him. 'Been shut down the cellar again. I'll let him out.'

I'd actually brought the dog home when his owner, a young

homeless man who'd been helping me trace someone, had died. I was ambivalent about keeping the animal but Ray and Digger hit it off.

I ushered the dog out of the back door and into the garden at the back. The sun was bright again and mist steamed off the grass, along the top of the garden fences and the roof of the shed. The dew had been heavy and swags of spider's web trailed silver beads among the foliage. I closed my eyes and drew in the air, cool and moist, felt a ripple of fatigue run through me. I took another breath and opened my eyes. Watched the coal tits on the bird feeder for a moment then dragged myself back inside.

In the cellar, I found Maddie's shorts and T-shirt. I put another load of dirty clothes in the machine, emptied the reusable nappies out of the bucket they were soaking in, holding my breath at the stink, and added those to the wash, sealing the velcro tabs carefully so they wouldn't claw at everything else.

Down there, beneath the kitchen, Jamie's crying was muffled and stopped suddenly; quiet followed. All I could hear was the water running into the machine and Digger's bark, asking to come in from the garden.

I went up to let him in and caught sight of the squirrel running along the fence. He'd already dug up most of the winter flowering bulbs I'd planted in a trough by the patio. I'd have loved to escape, stay out there and potter about: rake up the leaves and bag them for compost, clip back the bare lavender stalks and the straggly water mint that fringed the small pond. If only.

NINE

Diane lives in Fallowfield, a neighbourhood about a mile north of Withington, on the way into town. It's home to many of the city's students, who live in the purpose built halls of residence on Wilmslow Road and, behind the main drag, in the warren of small redbrick terraces. There's also a large council estate where generations of families have lived. Diane doesn't belong to either camp, though she's known and liked by her long-term neighbours who joke about her being their local Tracey Emin (though not half as successful).

Jamie's buggy doubled as a car seat, if you unhitched the top from the chassis. At Diane's house I got it out of the car, carried her in and put her down by the sofa.

Diane took a cursory glance at the baby, then folded her arms and looked at me. 'And you've no idea whose she is?'

'None. Look, here's the note. What d'you think that says?' I pointed to the signature.

She took the paper, peered at it. 'Lear? Lisa?'

'Isn't that an "H" at the beginning?'

'Or an "L"? Dunno. Waifs and strays, again, eh?' Diane thought I was too quick to jump in and rescue people.

'Hey, I didn't go out looking for her. And I could hardly send her packing.'

She nodded at the note. 'So have you told anyone?'

'No. Ray thinks I should.'

'How is the delectable Ray?'

The image of Ray scowling about Jamie was replaced in my mind by our impromptu afternoon sex. Something must have showed on my face because Diane hooted with laughter. 'Hah! Still steamy, huh? You're like a pair of teenagers.'

I smiled, fighting embarrassment. 'Like I say, he's not best pleased with our visitor – or how I'm handling it.' I checked my watch: time to go.

'How long will you be?' she asked warily. Diane is the most practical person I know: she hews wood, can build a kiln and fire pottery, erect scaffolding, bake cakes, weld metal. She can turn her hand to any sort of material but when faced with a small child she's a dead loss.

'A couple of hours max. She'll probably sleep for a while. If she starts to cry you add some boiling water to this.' I pulled out the bottle, which already had a feed in. 'Add about an inch, shake it, test it on your hand. Should be lukewarm.' Grabbing a cushion, I demonstrated. 'Hold her like this, bottle this way up.' I showed her the odd-shaped teat. 'She'll latch on. Let her have as much as she likes.'

'Burping and stuff?'

'Very good,' I teased. 'You've been swotting.'

Diane glared.

'Just hold her upright, pat her if you like, it's not essential. If she fills her nappy . . .'

Diane shot me a look.

'. . . I'll change her when I get back.' I'd promised Diane no nappies. I decided not to even mention vomit.

'Anything else?'

'If she wakes up you can talk to her.'

'What about?' She frowned.

I kept a straight face. 'Or just put her where she can see you while you get on with what you're doing.' I glanced around; usually Diane's latest project is evident from the state of the place but there were no sketches or paintings, boxes of fabric or reference books scattered about. 'What are you working on?'

'Resting.' Her description of the times between practical work when she cast about for new ideas. She had not long ago finished a triptych of mixed media pieces based on landscape photos from our holiday to Cuba together. The trip of a lifetime, made to celebrate Diane completing her cycles of chemo.

'I'll be as quick as I can,' I promised and left her to it.

The traffic was heavy and slow along Wilmslow Road, through Rusholme's Curry Mile. I distracted myself by gazing in the shop windows, picking out my favourite shalwar kameez, or comparing the fancy neon signs for the different restaurants and watching the pedestrians pass: students streaming in towards the universities, local people shopping for groceries, a group of women in richly patterned African dress, others in saris chatting to a shopkeeper in his flowing white galabiyya.

We crawled past the park and the infirmary, where a taxi and a bus got into a hooting competition after a near miss in the bus lane, on past the universities and the BBC building. Today the weather was muted. A change to neutral, the sky a hazy grey, blanketed with thick cloud; the trees still, the pavements muffled by the mush of crushed leaves.

I wasn't looking forward to meeting Damien Beswick again. He was awkward company and for all Chloe's efforts I wasn't sure that he'd be any more forthcoming than last time.

*   *   *

After passing through the gatehouse and the security checks, I was escorted to the same room. When Damien came in he looked tired: his eyes were pink, slightly bloodshot and he slumped into the chair. That nervy restlessness was still there, a foot tapping, his fingers moving to and fro, tracing the table's edge.

I got straight down to business. 'Chloe said you'd remembered something else.'

'I've been trying,' he said.

'And?'

He shrugged. I felt a lick of impatience. He looked shifty, scratched at his sideburn. 'I've tried,' he repeated. So it was a con. There's no stunning new evidence to support his claim to innocence, nothing new. He had wasted my time. I was on the brink of walking out but hated the thought of a wasted journey. Before calling it quits I would try out what I'd learned from Geoff Sinclair.

'Right,' I said brusquely. 'What I want to do is go over the events at the cottage in more detail. OK?'

He sighed. 'Yeah.'

'And what I want you to do,' I explained, 'is try and relax a bit; sometimes it is easier to remember if you don't force it.'

His eyes shone. 'Guinness Book of Records; there's this guy, he can remem—'

'Damien.' I cut him off. 'Do you want to do this?'

He closed his mouth tight, hands fisted; he rubbed one set of knuckles on the other. 'I don't like to think about it,' he said. His jaw was rigid, jutting forward, clenched emotion. 'It's in my head. I can't get it out of my head.' He wouldn't look at me.

'Do you need to see a doctor or a counsellor?'

'I've put a slip in.' I assumed that meant he'd requested an appointment. There was a long pause. 'I'll do it,' he said. 'Whatever you need. I didn't kill him.'

'It might help if you close your eyes.'

'You gonna hypnotize us?' A spark of humour.

'No.'

He let his head drop, folded his arms. A defensive move? Or protective?

'You were on the bus – think about that. You'd come from Sheffield. Was the bus busy?'

'Nah. Couple of old grannies, a girl with a little kid.'

'And you got thrown off?'

'I hadn't enough to get to Manchester. Thought the driver'd forgotten but he pulls in and turns the engine off. He's giving it out, blah, blah, blah. Comes up, wants my name and address.'

'What did he look like?'

Damien opened his eyes, looked at me.

'Think of it as practise, exercising your memory,' I said.

He rubbed his chin, let his head fall again. 'Fat bloke, glasses.'

'Good. What was he wearing?'

'Uniform?' It sounded like he was guessing.

'Only tell me what you can see, what you're sure about. Don't guess.'

'Can't remember,' he said.

'OK. You get off the bus. What's it like?'

'Freezing.' He folded his arms tightly.

'What else?'

'The wind's blowing. It's dark.'

'What are you wearing?' I asked.

'Jeans, sweat-top, jacket.'

'Good. What's in your pockets?' He didn't answer. 'Damien?'

'Some stuff: wrap of coke, a joint, lighter.'

Maybe that's why he hesitated. 'OK, what did you do next?'

'Took the stuff.' Something we hadn't covered last time. So maybe this was progress.

'The coke?'

'And the joint,' he said. 'I needed a little something, take the edge off.'

'Where were you while you did this?' Surely he'd not be in plain view.

'In the bus shelter.'

'Did you see anyone?'

'No.'

'Cars?'

'Some, not many.'

'Then what?' I was making notes as he spoke, writing quickly in a shorthand I've invented. It's a bit like text messaging – heavy on the consonants – but I also include sketches where that's useful.

'I needed some money, to get the bus. There were some places up the hill; I thought I'd check them out.'

'Why up the hill? That's away from the main road, isn't it?'

He raised his head. 'Yeah, but there's a pub along the bottom road, and a garage. There's going to be cameras. Don't wanna end up on *You've Been Framed*,' he said. 'But I have – been framed,' he added morosely.

You confessed, I wanted to point out, hardly a stitch up, but I stuck to my script – no diversions. 'You set off up the hill, what can you see?'

'Not much. Lights in the windows at one place up the hill.'

'You still cold?'

'Worse. Sometimes the weed'll do that,' he said, as if passing on a tip.

'Any noises?'

'Can't remember.'

'The drugs: how do they make you feel?' I said.

'Bit of a buzz, a lift.'

'Do they distort anything?' He'd been stoned; I wanted to know how that skewed his perception.

'It's only coke and weed,' he said derisively. 'Not like I'm on acid or shrooms.'

I nodded. 'Go on.'

'I passed the place with the lights on. Too risky. Checked the cars on the road, though; people leave change for parking, even if there's no valuables but they were locked. Immobilizers on.' The way he elaborated made me think he was actually remembering rather than making this up. That's what Sinclair had said: liars keep it simple, shorn of detail.

'What sort of cars?'

'A Mondeo and an old Volvo.' No hesitation – there for the asking. He laughed, his eyes flared with surprise. 'Sound, man.'

'Looks like it works,' I remarked. 'So, you pass the cars.'

'Go up and round the bend. There's a bloke coming down.'

'What's he wearing?'

He closed his eyes. 'A dark coat.'

'What else?' I said.

'Dunno.'

'Is he carrying anything?'

'No—' Damien broke off, corrected himself. 'A backpack.'

'Does he say anything?'

'No. He's in a hurry.'

'Walking fast?'

'Yeah. And . . . breathing hard.'

I wondered what the hesitation meant. Was he recovering the memory or fleshing out his phantom suspect for me? I needed to push and find out as much as I could about the man he claimed to have seen. 'Describe him?'

'Can't remember. Never really got a look at him, and I wasn't drawing attention to myself.'

'Was he taller than you?'

'No.'

'Smaller?'

'The same.' Again it sounded like a stab in the dark.

'You sure it was a man?'

'Yeah.'

'Why?'

'Dunno. The way he walked.' Damien shrugged, rolled back his head, eyes open.

'Black or white?'

'White.' He sounded definite.

What else could I ask? Sight, sound, touch . . . 'Did he smell?'

'Bit personal, innit?' he quipped, then the merriment in his face dissolved into something else. Sadness, fatigue. I wasn't sure where that had come from.

'Close your eyes,' I said. He did. 'Try to relax. You're going up the hill; you pass two cars, a Mondeo and a Volvo. You round the bend, he's coming down. You pass each other . . .' I waited.

'What's the point,' he complained, 'I can't remember.' His face was pinched, mouth trembling. 'You think I made him up. You're trying to trick me.' His voice rose. 'You don't believe me! Why d'you even bother coming back?' The outburst came out of the blue; a flash of temper but I didn't feel threatened.

'Shall I go?' I asked quietly.

In the silence I heard his breath stuttering. 'It's just hard. It's all fucking hard. I don't remember any more about him, only what I said already.' His voice was tight with frustration.

'OK. Carry on.'

He sighed.

'Damien,' I encouraged him, 'you're doing very well – you've told me a lot more than last time and it all helps. So, you pass this man, he's your sort of height, a white guy, dark coat, backpack and he's out of breath.' That last detail snagged in my mind but I didn't have time to consider it any further then. 'What next?'

'I go up a bit more and the cottage is there, set off up the road a bit. There's a car.'

'What sort?'

'Audi, on the drive. It's locked up. No lights at the house. I go up to the door, listen. Nothing from inside. Then an engine starts up somewhere and I wait to see if they're coming this way, but they don't. The windows are shut. I'm gonna check round the back but first I try the door and it just opens.' Damien swallowed.

'What can you see?'

'Nothing, it's too dark. I use my lighter.' He stopped. Breathed out noisily and put his head in his hands.

'Stay there,' I warned him, 'what can you see?'

'He's on the floor, a big guy, half on his side, one leg under him.'

'Show me.'

Damien looked askance but I tilted my head by way of invitation and he got up. He grinned self-consciously then positioned himself on the floor, left shoulder down, head twisted to the left so he was in profile. Left knee bent up underneath him, right arm across his stomach. Half foetal, half prone.

'OK,' I told him.

He got up, sat back in the chair, rubbed at his face. Closed his eyes without any prompting. 'I could see the blood, smell it. And the smell of shit.'

This was what Libby had found a couple of hours later, coming to meet her lover, running late, eager to tell him her good news: that they were having a child. The future full of promise. Opening the cottage door, snapping on the light. The shock, like a brick wall. Her world collapsing.

'What else do you remember?'

'I felt sick, nearly was sick there. I know the bloke's dead. I wanna get out of there.' Damien lowered his voice. 'I check his pockets.'

'Which ones?'

'Just his jeans, the one that's easy to reach, at the right, and his back pocket. Empty.'

'What does he feel like?'

He was outraged. 'What sort of question's that?'

'Was he cold, stiff?'

'I dunno,' he said hotly. 'I didn't touch him, innit?' Was his agitation because this was all make-believe and in truth Damien had stabbed Charlie then rooted through his clothes while the man lay dying? Or shame at scavenging from a corpse? Or some insecurity about his sexuality? That he'd been touching a man, and a dead man at that.

'Why are you so bothered by that?' I asked him.

His face closed down. 'I'm not,' he said flatly.

'What happened then?'

'I used the lighter to have a look round.' He sounded calmer.

'The cottage?'

'Just the kitchen. Seen the wallet on the worktop. Flick it open and there's tenners in there, some change. I'm out of there.'

'Wait,' I said.

'What?'

'Anything else in the room?'

'Car keys, next to the wallet.'

'You could have taken the car?' I was surprised he hadn't.

'Oh, yeah, and get stopped for dangerous driving,' he sneered.

'You a bad driver?'

'Never learnt. Couldn't afford to. It shows.'

'But you like cars; you remember the makes and models.'

'And?' he scowled.

Now I was the one veering off course. 'OK, in the kitchen – can you see a knife?'

'No.'

'But you knew he'd been stabbed?'

'All that blood. There was blood on his hands, on his shirt where he's holding his stomach, you know? His shirt is blue and yellow check but there's this massive patch on his front, on his sleeve. And the floor. Obvious. And they said on the news later—'

'Stick with what you actually saw. No knife?'

'No knife.'

'Then you came out . . .'

'Yeah, fast.'

'Did you shut the door?'

'Yeah, I think.'

It would make sense if he'd been running away; like Geoff Sinclair said, the impulse to hide the victim. 'And then?'

'Went for the bus—'

'Whoa! Slow it down.' He'd talked about being sick last time. And I expected him to have stronger sense memories after the shock of finding the body (or killing the man) than before. Adrenalin's a powerful hormone; it increases the heart rate and blood flow and primes us to fight or flee. Heightened sensory perception would be part of that response.

'You come out of the house. Close your eyes.'

'I was freaking, like it's some bad trip, I'm speeding, it's not real. Like I'm gonna pass out.'

'What else do you feel?'

'Cold.'

'Colder than in the house?'

'Yeah,' he said.

'Can you see anyone, hear anything?'

'No.' Then he corrected himself, adding quickly: 'Ticking.'

A clock? Inside his head. 'What?' I asked him.

'The car,' he said.

'The car's ticking?'

'Like it's cooling down.' He frowned, looking as puzzled as I felt. 'It was warm,' he went on slowly. 'I put my hand on it; I was gonna throw up. I put my hand on the bonnet.'

I couldn't work out what this meant but it seemed out of place. Not wanting to interrupt his flow I motioned for him to continue.

'Then I got to the gate and threw up. It was rank, man.'

'Then?'

'I go down the hill and sit in the bus shelter. I didn't see anyone. Some cars pass by and the bus comes and I get back into town. Go and score.'

Why didn't you report it if you really were innocent? I

wondered still. If the incident had shaken him as badly as he said, wouldn't he have been desperate to tell someone?

'The smell,' he said, 'that was the worst, and the blood. After that I was really using a lot, anything I could get down my neck, trying to wipe it out. I was in a bad place, a really bad place.' He began to rock as he talked, his arms wrapped tight about his stomach, another in the repertoire of his nervous tics but this spoke to me of a deeper trauma. 'I got slung out of the flat I was staying. Chloe didn't want to know. In the end, when the coppers picked me up and started going on about it, it just seemed easier to go along with it. Give them what they wanted and get rid. It could have happened like I told them. And they feed you in here, clothe you. That's where I was at. But it's not like that. Prison, it's—' He broke off. 'I can't do time.' He echoed the words from our first meeting. 'See that?' Urgently he pulled up his sleeve, revealed an angry gash, crusted with scabs, maybe half a centimetre wide, six or seven long on his forearm. 'Cut with a broken biro.'

'Who did it?'

'Me.' He rolled down his sleeve. 'That's how it gets you, you know.'

'But you've arranged to see the doctor?'

'Yeah,' he said dully, 'takes for ever. What now?' He nodded at my notes.

'I need to think about what you've told me.'

His face blanched. 'You still don't believe me?' He looked hurt.

'I've got more to go on than before. But it's not what I believe that matters; it's whether there is anything here that might stand as fresh evidence as far as the lawyers are concerned. That's what I need to work on.'

He didn't say anything else. He leant forward at the table, laid his head on his arms. Shattered or sulking. I put my head out and called the prison officer to take him back to his cell.

Collecting my mobile and car keys, I stepped back through the security centre and out of the prison. The outer gate clanged shut behind me and I walked across the car park to my car beneath the wide, bleak sky.

TEN

'How's she been?'

'Still asleep,' said Diane.

Jamie was exactly where I'd left her. While on the table, the sofa and around the edge of the carpet were large, thick sheets of drawing paper covered in charcoal sketches of the baby.

'Still life,' I observed. 'They're great.'

'Easy subject,' Diane said. 'Perfect artist's model. Like the quiff.' She referred to Jamie's spike of dark hair.

Some of the drawings showed Jamie and the carry-seat, others were close-ups. One I particularly liked: a very simple head and shoulders sketch, three-quarter profile, caught her exact likeness. I asked Diane if I could have it.

'To you, fifty quid,' she joked. 'Hang on.' She grabbed a spray can, got the picture from the sofa and disappeared into the backyard. I sat down. I could hear her rattling the aerosol, then the sibilance of the spray. Jamie stirred, her face working, legs twitching.

Diane brought the drawing back; there was a smell like glue. 'Fixative,' she said, 'to stop it smudging.' She moved the sketches from the sofa and put them with my one on the table. 'How was your meeting?'

Jamie opened her eyes and smacked her lips a couple of times. I reached down and stroked her cheek. 'Not sure – need to think it through.'

Diane cocked her head, interested.

'Remember the Charlie Carter murder? Man stabbed in his second home – in Thornsby.'

'A builder?' she checked.

'Yeah, he did loft conversions. The man I've just been to see confessed to the crime: he was caught with Carter's bank cards and the police could prove he was at the scene. But now he's saying he's innocent after all. And he's looking for grounds to launch an appeal.'

'So, what, you're working for his defence lawyer?' Diane knew more about my work than just about anyone, so she knew I often collect evidence and check statements for solicitors. Saves them the shoe leather.

'No,' I said, 'not that simple.' Jamie gave a little shriek and waved her fists about. 'I was hired by the dead man's lover who wants reassurance that the bloke behind bars should stay there.'

'Never a dull moment,' Diane smiled.

'I'd better make tracks.' I gestured at Jamie. 'She'll want feeding, then changing before long. Thanks for having her.'

I lifted the carry-seat and Jamie beamed at me. I caught sight of a crumb of something in her mouth and went to slip it out, running my finger along her gum. There was something hard, sharp. I peered closer, saw the translucent bluey bump, like a fragment of seashell. 'Oh, wow, look.' I turned to Diane. 'Her first tooth!'

Diane was looking at me, not the baby. She shook her head.

'What?' I asked her.

She shrugged. 'Don't you think you're getting a bit too involved?'

My face flushed with heat and I felt my pulse quicken. 'No!' I could hear how defensive I sounded. 'It's a milestone, that's all. You wouldn't understand.'

Diane regarded me steadily; it felt like a challenge.

I muttered something about having to go, and went.

Leaving the drawing behind.

I squabbled with the voices in my head all the way home and while I fed and changed Jamie. She was an engaging baby, pretty, reasonably settled given she'd been thrust into the care of strangers. What was I supposed to do? Keep her at arm's length, deny her any warmth or affection because she'd only be here a few days?

By the time I got round to making my own lunch I was ravenous, and hadn't resolved any of the edgy feelings that Diane's comment had awoken.

While I stirred a couple of blocks of frozen spinach and some spring onions into boiling water, I sifted through my reactions – trying to unpick the reasons behind them.

It was fair to say having Jamie had made me think anew about my relationship with Ray. And her appearance in my life had made me a little broody but that was a fancy, like window shopping, rather than a powerful driving need. True, I felt quite close to the child but wouldn't anyone who'd shared the isolation of broken nights and been the one she relied upon?

I'd seen some childcare guru on the telly who advocated keeping handling to a minimum, leaving babies alone apart from set feeding times, letting them cry if need be, in order to establish a fixed routine. She told stories of infants who slept for a straight ten hours at night, who never fussed or fretted. But that type of regime wasn't my style. It seemed cold and inflexible. And I'd be incapable of ignoring a crying child.

Was I too involved? Would I miss Jamie when she went? I scooped a spoonful of miso paste, made from fermented soya beans, mashed it with a little water and added it to my soup, sprinkling chilli flakes on top. Yes, I'd miss her a bit, but I had plenty of other stuff going on: I had a life, a job, a child, a lover, a business. I wasn't praying that Jamie would stay. I'd like to catch up on my sleep for starters. Realistically, even if her mother never returned, I wouldn't be able to keep her indefinitely. At some point I would have to inform social services.

I ate my broth with the last crust of home-made bread. When food prices had gone up we'd invested in a bread-making machine and never looked back. But the extra time the baby demanded had disrupted some of our everyday chores, like baking bread. I cleared my plates and got out the flour and yeast and seeds. I finally admitted to myself that my overreaction to Diane was because she'd put her finger on something I'd been trying to ignore. And rather than 'fess up and admit that the little girl had won me over and it would be a wrench when she went, I'd scrabbled to deny any such bond.

I took the baby round to the office with me, intent on working through my interview with Damien Beswick and making recommendations for Libby. It was chilly in the cellar room and I turned up the heating and switched on the table lamp. Before I started, I called Diane.

'Hey,' I said, 'sorry if I was a bit prickly back then. Felt like you and Ray were ganging up on me.'

'I don't want to see you get hurt,' she said.

'I won't. I can handle it. She's a nice baby, but that's all. Honestly. And I forgot the drawing.'

'I'll hang on to it for you.'

We said our goodbyes and I concentrated on the case. There were a number of items in Damien's account that interested me or raised questions – though I couldn't tell yet whether they had any bearing on establishing his guilt or innocence.

First, why had Charlie been in the cottage with the lights off but the door unlocked? If he'd gone for a sleep, surely he'd have locked up. If someone had been there before Damien (as he wanted me to believe) had that person switched off the lights when they were leaving? Why? A primal need to obscure what they'd done – in the same way that Damien had instinctively shut the door to hide the horror? After all, anyone coming to the cottage in the dark, like Libby, would be surprised to find the place in darkness. Leaving the lights on would actually make the place appear more normal, so attract less attention. As I mulled this over, I scribbled the gist of my ideas down in my notepad.

Damien had been uncomfortable when I asked him if he'd touched the body. What I'd been trying to find out was whether Charlie's skin was cool to the touch – or warm. It would be in the police case notes; the pathologist called to the scene would have taken the temperature of the victim and estimated time of death. Maybe Geoff Sinclair would be able to remember? I made a note to phone him. Charlie couldn't have been there for very long; he'd not left home till four.

The second thing that puzzled me was Damien's description of Charlie's car: how it had been ticking as the metal contracted, how the bonnet felt warm. Cars cool down pretty quickly anyway and it was November time so the temperatures would be lower; that suggested that Charlie had used it very shortly before his death, before Damien arrived.

Third was Damien's 'walker'. The passer-by with the rucksack. The only living soul that Damien admitted seeing from getting off the bus to climbing on board again later. Sinclair said the police had no knowledge of this character. But in the days after the murder, they would have crawled all over the village, interviewing anyone home or in the area that day and cross-referencing everybody's accounts. Appeals had been made for witnesses: *'Anyone who saw anything, no matter how small, no matter how insignificant or irrelevant it may seem, please let us know.'* And at that stage it would be another two weeks until Damien Beswick was apprehended.

So imagining this man existed, if he was an innocent bystander, he walked past the cottage on the very day that a brutal murder was carried out. He went home after his walk or whatever, had a shower, made his tea. The next day on the telly, or in the papers he read how close he was. Why not call it in? Maybe he didn't notice Damien and so thought he had nothing to tell the enquiry. Maybe he got home that evening and changed for his holiday in New Zealand or wherever, and flew off and missed the brouhaha.

Or he kept quiet, lay low, because he wasn't innocent, he hadn't been up in the hills walking – he'd been killing Charlie. And he'd left the cottage moments before Damien arrived. Damien's description was pretty vague but one detail that he had recalled without my prompting was that the man had been out of breath, panting, which would fit if you were hurrying away from a murder scene, though it would fit equally well if you were an energetic fell walker coming down the hills at the end of a hard day's tramp. And he had been lugging a backpack with him.

If this was a suspect, what was his motive? Nothing was stolen apart from the wallet that Damien took. There weren't any other suspects, unless . . . My mind darted back to the old business partner that Libby had mentioned: the alcoholic who bore a grudge even though he'd been the one dragging the firm to the edge of insolvency. I flicked through my notes: Nick Dryden. Had something happened that made him suddenly act many years after things had turned sour? Was there some personal crisis that had tipped him over the edge from angry drunk to homicidal maniac? How would he know where to find Charlie? Charlie wasn't at home. Had Dryden been stalking him and followed him to the cottage? I shook my head at the image that conjured up: the little convoy setting out on a winter's afternoon. Charlie in front heading for Thornsby and looking forward to seeing Libby; behind him Valerie driving Heather, the anxious wife looking for evidence to prove her suspicions, and after them Nick Dryden, out for blood.

I gave up on work. I would ring Sinclair the following day, see what he could tell me about the estimate for Charlie's time of death, how warm the body was and if they had made any efforts to trace Nick Dryden and find out where he'd been the day Charlie was killed.

Maddie was in full strop from the moment she came out of school. It's never a good time of day – I know she's often tired and hungry and cranky so I made allowances when she slung her lunch box under Jamie's buggy and it flew open, spilling wrappers and a squashed up drink carton. And when she refused to put her coat on and walked home shivering, going blue around the gills.

I made them some toast and hot chocolate and thought things would improve. They scoffed it at the kitchen table, where Jamie was sitting in her seat.

'Jamie's got her first tooth,' I told them.

'Let's see.' Tom stood up and craned his neck, as I gently pulled Jamie's lower lip down. Maddie refused to be impressed. Maddie was jealous. The first flush of interest in the baby had given way to feeling usurped.

'Feel it with your finger,' I suggested. He did and Jamie clamped her mouth shut.

'She bit me!' He didn't know whether to be cross or delighted but I could tell he wasn't hurt. 'It's sharp.'

Maddie went off to the living room and Tom peered at his finger for a moment, then ran after her.

'Stop following me,' I heard her snap.

'I'm not. I just want to watch telly.'

'Well, you can't. You always talk,' she said.

'I do not!' Tom protested.

'Liar!'

Maddie wasn't getting enough attention and behaving badly was a sure-fire way of attracting lots of it. Before it could get any heavier I intervened and they settled down in front of the box. But ten minutes later, while I was feeding Jamie, there was an almighty crash from the living room. I pulled the bottle out of her mouth and hurried to see what was going on.

The television was face down on the floor. Maddie looked flushed and guilty. Tom was crying.

'He was in the way,' Maddie said sulkily. 'I told him to move.'

'I was not,' Tom shouted, furious with passion and his face dark, snot bubbling out of his nose. 'She kept getting closer.'

Jamie began to cry.

'She kept pushing me. She pushed me into the telly and—'

'He pulled it down,' Maddie said quickly.

'It fell down!' Tom screamed.

'All right.' I plonked the baby on the sofa and held up both my hands.

'He's trying to blame it on me,' Maddie insisted.

'Shush,' I told her as I knelt and unplugged the television.

'You always take his side,' Maddie shouted now and ran upstairs. Tom was sobbing and Jamie was howling.

I moved and gave Tom a hug. He usually came off worse when the kids fell out. Maddie was more calculating, devious even, and Tom couldn't bear the injustice. She'd engineer an argument or a fight and then try to seize the moral high ground. Being a year older, and a girl, also made her more articulate and she'd confuse him and trip him up with the way she put a spin on things. It wasn't a trait I liked in my daughter and I guess, like many parents, there were times when I wondered whether I'd done anything to encourage it.

'We'll talk about it properly when you've both calmed down,' I told Tom.

'Is it broken?' He took his arms from round my neck; his dark eyes were wide and soft and shiny with tears. He winced as Jamie's cries reached glass-shattering pitch.

'I don't know. I'd better finish feeding Jamie and then I'll have a look.'

He swiped at his face with both hands.

'You go blow your nose,' I said, 'and stay away from Maddie for a bit.'

The crying had given Jamie hiccups and it took twice as long to feed her. She filled her nappy, again, and the contents were particularly virulent, probably to do with her teething. She didn't show any signs of going to sleep once I'd wrested her into clean clothes, so I peeled a piece of carrot for her, large enough so she couldn't choke on it, and gave her it to gnaw on. If the tooth was hurting her at all maybe it would help. She took to it straight away, making little droney sounds.

The telly was dead. When I plugged it in the stinky smell of burning plastic filled the room. Tom was in the playroom bashing together a pair of action men – probably imagining dispatching Maddie in various gruesome ways.

'Now tell me what happened,' I said, clearing a pile of wooden bricks and bits of plastic from the floor so I could sit down.

He clutched the dolls as he talked only making eye contact with me at crucial points. 'We were watching Basil Brush and Maddie said I was in the way but I wasn't. I moved a bit and then she sat in front of me and I couldn't see anything and I sat closer and she tried to push me out of the way and I pushed her then I got up and she pushed me again. And I fell on the telly and then it fell down. I'm sorry, Sal.'

'OK.'

Maddie was in her bed, hidden by the covers.

'Maddie, sit up.'

She made me wait but did eventually emerge from the duvet, looking as defiant as she could.

'Tell me what happened?'

'I told you,' she said. 'Tom was in the way and he wouldn't move. I couldn't see. He kept doing it and then he knocked the telly off.' She looked miserable but her jaw was set and her chin lowered so she was glowering at me.

'And what did you do?'

'Nothing,' she said brusquely. She ground her teeth mutinously.

'Maddie, tell me the truth.'

'I am!' she cried.

'All of it.'

'That is all of it.'

I worked very hard at not losing my temper with her. 'I don't think Tom got up and pulled the telly over on purpose; I think something happened between you first. Did you push Tom?'

'He pushed me, too.'

'So that's a yes.'

She gave a little sigh and her shoulders slumped.

'It's important to tell the truth, Maddie. If Tom got told off, or you did, for something you hadn't done, that wouldn't be fair, would it?'

'No.' Her voice couldn't get any smaller.

'If Tom was in the way, what else could you have done?'

'Got you.'

'Yes. Because getting into a pushing competition means that the telly is broken and neither of you will be able to watch anything until we can afford to buy a new one. And that might be quite a while,' I added, wanting her to understand that she'd suffer as a result.

Maddie's face had gone blank now, as if she was trying to absent herself from the situation.

From downstairs Jamie gave a cry and Maddie groaned. 'When's she going home?'

'I don't know when Jamie's going home,' I answered her. 'I know it's not very easy having a baby here, is it?' She didn't say anything, so I carried on. 'But the telly is broken and I think you should say sorry.'

'Sorry,' she said ungraciously and fell back flat on the bed. 'Can you go now?'

And that was as good as it got.

Ray was furious about the telly but I persuaded him not to talk to the kids until he'd calmed down a bit. Yelling at them wouldn't achieve much. 'I think Maddie's jealous of the baby,' I said. 'I think that's why she was winding Tom up. And he was really upset – don't be too hard on him.'

'They can't just get away with murder,' he said. 'What's that going to cost? Two hundred quid? Three?'

I shrugged. 'We don't have to replace it immediately.'

'Are we covered by accidental damage?'

'Maybe, but the excess will be a couple of hundred to start with.'

He sighed. 'So, I'll have to watch the match at the pub,' he complained.

I hadn't given any thought to football – nothing new there. 'When's it start?'

'Seven forty-five.'

'We need formula,' I said. 'Can you hang on until I get back? She's asleep now,' I said, moving to pick up my purse, trying to get out of there before he started on again about Jamie and what I should or shouldn't do.

'Sal, it's been four days—'

'I can count.' I pulled on my coat and left.

There's a mini-market on the main road and I thought it was big enough to carry different brands of baby milk. People were still commuting home from work; it was dark already and foggy now. The mist diffused the street lights into fuzzy globes and car headlights picked out skeins of fog, like soft grey netting. The air was ripe with exhaust fumes and the smell of fat-frying from the chippie.

As I pushed the heavy shop door open, I met a woman coming out. She looked familiar from school, though I didn't know her well. Her son had been in Tom's class but had changed schools the previous year. She remembered me, though, and stepped back into the shop. 'Sal? Jenny. How are you? Tom OK?'

'Yes.'

I couldn't ask after her boy as I'd forgotten his name but she went on regardless. 'Piers still asks after him. We'll have to get them together. Tom must come for tea sometime.'

'Yes, he'd like that.' I hoped, if it ever came to pass. 'Does Piers like the new school?'

'Loves it, thank God. And we're near enough so he can walk.' She hefted her bag of shopping from one hand to the other. 'So, how's Laura?'

'Laura?' Ray's ex. The one he'd finished with in order to start his dalliance with me. I'd felt bad about it; I liked her but at least Ray had been honest and not tried to deceive anyone.

Jenny grinned. 'Did she have a boy or a girl?'

'Sorry?' I said stupidly. My throat felt dry and my stomach lurched.

'I saw her at the open-air theatre – Wythenshawe Park. We must have had the only dry day in March. She looked fit to pop. Didn't get chance to talk.'

My mind was fracturing. I heard myself speak, sounding quite normal: 'They split up, Ray and Laura. I've not seen her.' Meanwhile I was doing sums in my head, seeing that it added up and a voice was shouting: Laura's pregnant, Laura's had a baby. Ray's baby. Ohgod, ohgod, ohgod.

'Oh, sorry, I'd no idea,' Jenny said. 'Can't be easy for her.'

'No.' I wanted to push her out of the shop and shut her up.

'Keep in touch.' She nodded.

I mirrored her and stood back and watched her leave.

She reminds me of Tom, Ray had said about Jamie. My ears were buzzing, the strip light flickering above hurt my eyes and I felt sick and cold. The signature on the note: not *Lisa* or *Lear* but *Laura*. Oh, God.

The baby hadn't been left for me, but for Ray. Jamie was Ray's daughter. His and Laura's. *He* was supposed to look after her, not me. It all fit.

And I began to shake.

ELEVEN

My heart wouldn't stop hammering as I raced to grab the formula then fumbled to find my purse and pay. I dropped my change, picked it up and knocked over the tub of baby milk. The checkout girl laughed sympathetically but my jaw was clenched too tight to smile back.

There was no way I could go straight home: I was too upset, too confused. My mind was humming and fuzzy with the news I'd heard.

Diane opened the door. 'You've come for your drawing?' Then she saw my face. She didn't ask, didn't say a word. Just opened her arms and drew me in.

She listened as I explained the situation. 'So she's Laura's baby, and Ray's,' I finished. My phone rang. I knew it would be Ray, pacing the hall, eager to leave for the pub. I didn't answer it.

'You can't be certain,' she cautioned.

'No. But it's pretty bloody likely. Maybe I'm overreacting but it just feels like it'll change everything. He'll waltz off into the sunset with Laura and Tom and Jamie and . . . I can't stand this!' Suddenly I was angry rather than sad; the aching sensation in my guts replaced by a spike of rage. 'When did I get to be so needy? I don't want to depend on Ray for how I'm feeling; I don't want my happiness, my sanity, to be in his hands.'

Diane just gave me one of her looks; the cynical one that reads 'get real'. 'Look, them ending up together isn't likely, is it?' She pointed out. 'They've been apart for almost a year. She never even told him she was pregnant, or that he was going to be a father; not exactly happy-ever-after material. And he loves you, doesn't he?'

'But they've got a child together.' I was thinking of how Ray was with Tom and couldn't imagine him not wanting to be involved with Jamie once he knew.

'Well, there isn't a thing you can do about that but you don't know how it'll play out. You're imagining the worst but anything could happen. Maybe she'll give Ray custody and you two will raise the kid; maybe that's why she's left her with Ray now. Or maybe Laura will move away with the baby and Ray won't ever see her again. It's all maybes.'

'We still don't know why she left the baby,' I conceded.

'Exactly – or whether it is hers.'

My phone rang again. Ray would be tearing his hair out. Let him. I realized how cross I was with him, jealous as if he was culpable for this mess. Of course, biologically he was part of the equation but he was still ignorant that he had a daughter. I knew I wasn't being fair or logical – it was beyond me at that point.

'Coffee, cake?' Diane stood up.

It would have been lovely to stay, drinking strong coffee made with hot milk and the rich, dark chocolate cake that she always had on the go. But I knew I had to pull myself together and get on with it.

'You'll be OK,' Diane said as she saw me out. 'It'll work out. But anything you need . . .'

I nodded, gave her a farewell hug and got in the car.

Halfway home it hit me that I'd forgotten the sketch of Jamie. Again. Intentionally this time? Was I really that shallow? I was chastened to find that my attitude to the baby had shifted a little. No longer simple and instinctive but cluttered with complex, half understood emotions. Because she wasn't a foundling without any background or parents but connected to Ray and Laura and to a prior relationship that threatened me.

Ray was in the hall, Jamie fretting in his arms when I came in the door. Father and daughter.

'Finally.' He gave me a disgusted look. 'Here, she's been grizzling since you left.' He thrust her into my arms.

'Ray—'

'The match.' He pulled his jacket on. 'I've missed twenty minutes.'

'Sod the match. This is important.' My tone was steely and he halted momentarily.

'What can possibly be more important? Tell me later.' He moved to the door.

'The baby. She's yours,' I blurted out. 'Yours and Laura's.'

He frowned, gave a little laugh as if I'd caught him out with a practical joke, then his grin collapsed in on itself and his eyes drilled into me. 'What?' His face was raw with disbelief, pale with shock.

'Come and sit down.'

In the sitting room, I looked at the telly, at Ray's expression and wondered flippantly what the third catastrophe would be. I settled Jamie on my lap, used a finger to rub at her gums. Ray didn't speak while I recounted what the woman in the shop had said.

'It's possible, isn't it?' I asked him. 'Dates-wise.'

'Just.' His voice sounded dry, dusty.

'And remember you noticed that Jamie looked like Tom as a baby.'

He glanced sideways at Jamie.

'You'd no idea Laura was pregnant?'

His face narrowed and his eyes blazed. 'How can you ask me that? For chrissakes, Sal, don't you think I'd have mentioned it?'

'The note.' I slung Jamie over my shoulder and went and

fetched the slip of paper; thrust it in front of him. 'Is that Laura's signature?'

'No.' But he didn't sound certain.

'Are you sure?'

He didn't answer.

'You'll have to go see her, talk to her.'

He bent over, elbows on his knees, head in his hands, his fingers grasping his curls, and groaned.

Jamie began to cry and I walked to and fro, patting her on the back.

Ray looked up at me. 'I don't know if I still have her number.'

'Go round there, then,' I said. 'Go now, turn up on her door-step. See how she likes it,' I muttered. I gritted my teeth together, fighting the burning at the back of my eyes.

He gave a big sigh and got up. He looked tired and shaken. Jamie kept crying. Ray made no move towards me. Didn't say anything as he walked out, leaving me holding the baby.

Preoccupied and finding it hard to settle Jamie, I let Maddie and Tom do the minimum to get ready for bed. A wipe of hands and face, brush teeth and change.

Maddie was giving me the silent treatment, which was rather overshadowed by the baby's bleating.

'I'll come and read you a story as soon as Jamie's gone down,' I promised them.

'Yippee!' Tom dive-bombed into his bed, forgetting for the umpteenth time that he wasn't allowed to. The cheap pine frame had already been mended with brackets where he'd cracked it. With his usual resilience and even temper, Tom had recovered from the upset over the TV. Unlike Maddie, who would remember it to her dying day and feel wronged, whether she had been or not.

'No jumping on the bed,' I told Tom. 'I'll be back soon.'

I put them a Ms Whiz story CD on and turned off the overhead light. If Jamie was Tom's little sister, I expected he'd adapt to the situation equably. But Maddie? And me?

Jamie took some of a bottle, and while she fed I examined her for signs of Ray or Laura. Her eyes were greeny-brown, not conker coloured like Ray's and his son's. Laura had pale eyes, grey. Jamie's hair was dark – what she had of it – but straight, not curly. It could change, of course, become curly or turn blonde like Laura's. The baby's skin was pale, rosy; closer to Laura's shade than Ray's olive complexion. I remembered Laura had a small brown birthmark on one cheek but there was nothing like that on Jamie. Then again, I wasn't sure whether such marks were usually inherited.

Jamie fussed over the bottle now. I stopped feeding her and checked her nappy. It was damp and she squalled loudly while I changed her. I buttoned up her Babygro and took her with me to sit in the rocking chair in the kitchen. I rocked and sang to her all the nursery rhymes that came without effort: Old King Cole, The Grand Old Duke of York, Pop Goes the Weasel, Daisy Daisy, Lavender Blue and Bye Baby Bunting. I was focusing on the here and now, trying to quieten my chattering mind and lose myself in the sensations: the creak of the wooden runners, the heavy dull ache in my back and shoulder, the hot weight of the baby's body against my chest, the creamy smell of her, her breath damp on my neck.

She fell asleep. I kept the rocking up for a while then slowed and stopped. Carefully as possible I struggled to my feet and tensed against her waking, but she slumbered on and stayed like that as I crept upstairs and stooped to put her in the travel cot.

The children were asleep, too. Tom on his tummy with one leg flung clear of the duvet and Maddie curled on her side; beside her on the bed was a book she must have picked out for me to read. She had tried to stay awake hoping I'd come, looking forward to something to redeem the lousy day. My eyes prickled and I felt a pang of guilt. Another black mark. It felt like everything was warping, turning sour, coming adrift.

Downstairs I poured myself a large glass of Cabernet Sauvignon, an Australian brand that the Co-op had on offer at three for a tenner.

I ran a deep bath and sprinkled in some rose and geranium salts that Diane had bought me for my birthday. The water was hot and the scent was heady: the sweetness of the rose tempered by the darker, pungent scent of geranium.

In the bath, I took a huge swig of my wine, savouring the

berry flavours, then lay back and tried to get things in perspective. It wasn't easy: for every positive thought I had like 'we're all adults, we can work something out' there was an equally negative one like 'Ray will see Laura with his daughter and realize how wrong he's been to let her go'.

I took another drink, then the first piercing wail reached me. Jamie was awake and I dragged myself out of the water to go and tend to her. If Ray is the father, I thought to myself, he can bloody well do the nights from now on.

It was eleven thirty and I was in bed but wide awake when I heard him come back. The door banged a second time; he'd be taking Digger for his walk.

I'd left a note on the kitchen table asking him to see me when he came in. I was taut with apprehension, my guts twisted in knots. Unable to stay still, I got out of bed and put my dressing gown and slippers on and went to wait on the stairs.

What would he say? I tried to imagine but failed. What would it mean? My eyes roamed over the pictures on the walls: a photograph of the city, some of the kids' paintings, two of Diane's silk-screen prints, and took in the carpet on the stairs, threadbare in places. I looked down at the hallway that needed a tidy up and a lick of paint. Home. And it all felt precious and tenuous. If Ray left, could I cope here? Rebuild a sense of family with someone new, a stranger? Only recently we'd talked about renting out the attic flat again – we could use the money. Our experience with lodgers had been mixed but more good than bad. But if Ray went, I'd need to let out Ray's room as well as the flat. Perhaps convert the playroom into another bedroom as well. I'd be in a minority; the new people would invariable bring their own foibles and habits. New debates about the standard of housework and how we shared the kitchen. Could I face all that again? Maybe it was time to call it a day. To leave the lovely old house and the garden I'd spent hours creating and all the memories, and find somewhere manageable for Maddie and me. What could I get for the same rent? A rabbit hutch with a window box.

The sound of the door opening snapped me back to the present. Ray came in with Digger. He took the lead off the dog. He saw me sitting on the stairs and looked away while he shrugged off his jacket.

'Well?' My voice sounded small in the space.

'No one there.'

'What?'

'No one in. No answer. No lights on.'

The anticlimax was infuriating. 'Well, didn't you try the neighbours? Ask if she'd moved or something?'

'I'm not the bloody detective,' he swore at me. 'It's still her name on the buzzer.'

'Well, we can't just leave it like this,' I protested. 'We need to know, Ray.'

'I know!' he shouted back at me, flinging his arms wide. 'But there's nothing I can do till tomorrow. I'll go back then, all right?'

'Shit.' I got to my feet and stomped up the stairs. Then a thought hit me. I turned round and came down a few steps. 'Where've you been?' It was classic and could have been lifted from any movie – the nagging wife and the errant spouse. 'You'd have been there by eight. So where did you go after?'

Ray shook his head slowly, mouth ajar, in a gesture that proclaimed how breathtakingly unacceptable my questions were.

'You went to the pub!' I accused him. 'I'm sat here like an idiot, desperate to know if you're the father of this baby and you swan off to watch the match. That's how much it matters to you. You didn't even call me!'

He walked away from me. I was livid. I whirled around and ran back to my room. As I opened my door, I realized there was something else he needed to know. I marched downstairs and into the kitchen. He was making coffee. He turned to look at me, his face closed, chin raised, ready to defend himself. Guilty as sin.

I wagged a finger in true harridan style. 'And when that baby wakes up,' I spat at him, 'I'll bring her to you and you can damn well sort her out.' I jabbed my finger at him one final time, for emphasis.

Back in bed the frustration and sense of impotence seethed inside me like food poisoning. The froth of indignation rose high in my chest. I hoped he'd come and explain, ask for my understanding, comfort me. Soothe away the awful anger I felt and the fear that flickered beneath it. But before long I heard Ray go to bed and the snick of his door closing, like a reproach.

Sleep came at last with lurid, twisting dreams. Houses melting and merging, swept away by a raging torrent of water, corridors swaying and plunging, doorways shrinking and me dragging Maddie along, finding myself lost in unfamiliar rooms and hidden attics, as the building buckled and fractured, as the flood rose.

And Jamie slept right through.

The day was thick with fog; the air smelt sour and matched my mood. It was the weekend so the kids would rise late. Even Jamie slept until seven thirty.

Before I got downstairs, I heard Ray call Digger and take him out. I was relieved not to have to face Ray while I fed the baby and got my breakfast. Was he the same? Sneaking out to avoid me? The issues between us were too prickly.

Maddie came down and helped herself to Weetabix. Jamie had hiccups again. I thought Maddie might be amused but I'd not allowed for her growing disdain for the interloper. She cast a scornful glance at the baby, her lip curling in an impressive sneer.

'What would you like to do today?' I asked her. Even though I knew my day would be dominated by Ray's return visit to Laura's and the consequences.

Maddie shrugged.

I cast about for suggestions. Tried a few: 'The park, the cinema, baking?'

'The Arndale,' she proposed, with a pleased little nod.

I hated shopping malls as much as she loved them. 'Perhaps,' I said weakly.

She smiled.

'But we won't stay long. Is Tom still asleep?'

'Yes – and he's snoring.'

'Well, see if he wants to come when he wakes up.'

'I'll wake him!' She dashed out.

'Maddie—' I called to stop her but she ignored me, her feet drumming up the stairs.

Ray got back from walking the dog. I steeled myself as he came into the kitchen.

'Ray, I was thinking,' the words were clotted in my mouth, 'Laura's number – someone where she works might give you it.'

'It's personal information,' he said coldly, peering into the cupboard, 'they'll hardly hand it out on spec.'

'I just thought—'

'Christ, Sal!' He slammed his hand on the counter. 'I'm going round there, I told you last night. Just give me chance.'

'Don't shout at me!' I yelled.

Digger barked and skittered into the kitchen, ready to defend his lord and master. Jamie jerked; startled by the noise, her lip began to tremor. My phone rang.

I swore and picked it up, slid it open. 'Hello.'

'It's Chloe.'

My heart sank. I didn't want to talk to her or discuss her flaky brother's chances at the moment. 'Chloe, this really isn't a good time,' I said quickly. 'Can I ring you Monday?'

'It's Damien,' she said, her voice odd. Then, in a rush: 'He's dead. They found him hanging in his cell this morning.' And her voice cracked. 'He's killed himself. He's gone and killed himself.'

TWELVE

Chloe's house was busy with well-wishers. Neighbours or family, I'm not sure. No one introduced me. There was an atmosphere of shock, accompanied by that sudden intimacy of strangers in the wake of any disaster.

'Is she here?' I asked the woman who answered the door.

'In the back.'

I went through the living room, where the hum of conversation was louder than the muted TV. Chloe's kids were there in front of the set, another child beside them and on the sofa and assorted chairs maybe half-a-dozen people.

There were people crammed in the kitchen and others smoking in the backyard. Chloe was seated in the same place at the kitchen table. She looked up, relieved to see me, and someone stood up to give me their seat.

Chloe looked washed out, her eyes red-rimmed. Like Damien's had been.

'I'm so sorry,' I told her, 'it's a terrible thing.'

She nodded, biting her lip, and then sniffed hard. 'I can't believe it,' she said, her mouth working. 'The stupid—' She hit at her forehead with the heel of her hand. I put a hand out and caught her wrist. Felt the heat there.

'How was he?' she asked me. 'You saw him.'

I recalled Damien's fingers dancing on the table, his mercurial shifts of attitude. 'Restless. He told me more than he had done before, remembered more.'

'Did he say anything?'

I knew what she was asking. I cleared my throat; my mouth felt dry. 'He said he couldn't get it out of his head. And that he couldn't do time. But he'd booked to see a doctor.' That last image of him: his head on the table, drained. *You don't believe me*, he'd shouted. I hurried on. 'Chloe, if I'd had any idea.'

She raised her hand to stop me. 'He was only twenty-two,' she said. 'Barely a man. His whole life—'

Someone behind me murmured agreement.

'I still want to clear his name.' Chloe stared at me. 'Did he tell you anything new? Stuff we can use?'

I hesitated. 'Bits and bobs. I'm not sure.'

A change came over her face and she drew back a fraction, her eyes hardening. 'You don't believe him,' she accused. The atmosphere in the room bristled and people stilled. I could hear people talking outside and someone coughing.

'You can deal with all this later, Chloe,' an older woman spoke gently. 'You've enough on.'

Chloe ignored her. 'Well?' she asked me.

'I don't know.'

'Well, I do.' She was shaking. She took a breath. 'He left a note, right. A note saying he didn't do it. That he was innocent and he just couldn't stand it any more.' She blinked and tears splashed from beneath her lashes. She wiped them away with both hands and blew her nose on a tissue. 'That's proof,' she said hoarsely. 'You're not going to lie about something like that if you're going to end it all, innit.'

'It counts for a lot,' I agreed. Deathbed confessions do carry weight. People don't want to depart the world wreathed in lies.

'Will you see his lawyer; tell her what he told you?'

'Yes.'

That satisfied her. Someone put a mug of coffee in front of her and a pack of tablets. 'There'll be an inquest, sometime,' she said. 'They'll want to talk to you.'

'Yes.'

I thought of all she had to deal with: registering the death, the funeral arrangements, collecting his possessions from the prison. And Damien's mother – would she know about her son's death? Was she still alive herself?

There was knocking at the front door, then voices, business-like. A man came through from the living room. 'Chloe? It's the BBC, local news. Want to know if they can talk to you.'

Chloe thought for a second and made her decision. 'Yeah, bring 'em in.'

Should I have been able to tell how fragile Damien's state of mind was? Wouldn't the prison officers, his fellow inmates, be better placed? They'd seen him every day; I'd visited twice. I didn't want to blame myself. But no matter how determined I was not to get into any guilt trips there was some fickle part of my soul that was whispering in the wind: mea culpa, mea culpa, mea culpa. *You're trying to trick me*, he'd yelled. *I can't do time.* The weal on his arm. *You don't believe me.*

Would it have made any shred of difference if he'd left that room thinking I did?

Libby was still my client and I needed to let her know what was happening, to talk to her before she came across it on the news. She was doing a site visit at Tatton Park, a large estate with a stately home, a deer park and an impressive lake fifteen miles to the south of the city. She'd be there for the next hour and a half but after that had a family lunch to get to. It made sense for me to drive down and meet up with her there.

We rendezvoused in one of the car parks inside the park. The rolling heath land was planted with stands of Scots pine and broadleaf trees, shrouded in mist. The air was cool and moist and smelt of damp wool. I got out of my car and Libby waved me over to hers. A few hundred yards away three large marquees were being erected. Trucks stood by with more scaffolding and planking which would be used for the floors.

Libby suggested we sit in her car; she had Rowena in the back. 'I don't often bring her out but she sleeps mornings regular as clockwork. Don't know what I've done to deserve that.' She smiled.

The baby was a similar age to Jamie but physically very different: solid and chubby, with a bald head. There wasn't space in my head to think about Jamie, about the situation at home. It lurked there, a tight ball in my guts, a pressure at the back of my skull.

'Takes after Charlie.' Libby smiled again. 'Rugby player.'

'Did he play?'

'Nah. Just built like one. Liked to watch. That and motor racing. Liked to put his foot down. He always said he had enough exercise lugging stuff about at work. You said you had some news?'

'Yes. I'm afraid it's bad news, about Damien Beswick. Sad, too. Damien committed suicide last night.'

'Oh, my God.' Her hand flew to her face.

'I saw him yesterday,' I said. 'We went over his new version of events. He was reasonably cooperative. He maintained he didn't attack Charlie. And he left a note, last night, saying the same.'

'What does this . . . I don't know what this means,' she said quickly, thumping the steering wheel with one fist. 'Are you saying he didn't do it?' Her face was mobile with confusion.

'It's more likely that he's innocent than it was before,' I said. A plane flew overhead, coming in to land at the airport close by.

She glared at me. 'Did they know he might do this? Had he tried anything before?'

'He was unsettled. He'd self-harmed. He was on some medication to calm him down. But his sister implied he had access to illegal stuff, too. She says the drugs made him worse but he found it hard to cope without them. But he wasn't considered to be a suicide risk, no. I saw him yesterday and it never crossed my mind that he'd do something like this.'

There was movement in a copse to our right and a pair of red deer, large with huge antlers, walked into view. They seemed like creatures from another age.

'And his version: did it add up?'

'Possibly. At the very least there were some inconsistencies that I'd like to look at again and talk to the police about. I did go to see Geoff Sinclair but that was before this.' What would he make of Damien Beswick's sudden death? 'Even if you don't want me to carry on,' I said to Libby, 'I'll be passing on what I know to the authorities.'

'Well, I can't just leave it like this,' Libby said. 'Not knowing. If he was innocent then that's two lives lost, not just Charlie. And if they got it wrong, if it wasn't him, then who was it?'

'I don't know. Look, Nick Dryden, did the police ever talk to him?'

She stared at me. 'I've no idea. You think he might have done it?'

I watched the deer move off, silhouetted against the sky as they crested a slope. 'He's the only enemy that's ever been mentioned. He should be ruled out.'

'Can you find out?'

'I can see what Geoff Sinclair knows.'

She sat back, resting her head on the head brace, her face tilted up. 'Can they reopen the case with Damien dead?'

'I imagine it will be harder but not impossible. It'll be easier if there are enough grounds to try someone else.'

'What a mess.' She shook her head. 'How did he . . .?'

'He hung himself.'

She shuddered and shifted in her seat. 'Do what you can.'

I opened the door and got out of the car. Then bent down as another thought occurred to me. 'The press might be back.'

She groaned. 'Oh, God. Yeah. OK.'

As I shut the door, I could see a group of fallow deer making their way down to the lake. The expanse of water lay blurred by the mist: a steely grey reflecting the sky above. Ducks swam and cormorants posed still as stone on the palings near the shore. But even the sombre weather didn't dampen the brilliant flare of ginger and purple in the patches of heather and the blaze of copper in the trees across the lake.

*   *   *

I drove home via Hale. I had no obligation to Heather and Alex Carter; nevertheless, I felt I ought to show my face and see if they had heard the news. It wouldn't be easy for them. No matter how sure they were about Damien's guilt, his deathbed confession – or retraction to be precise – would disrupt any sense of closure they had. Everything would float to the surface again. I had an ulterior motive, too: Heather Carter would know more about Nick Dryden than Libby. And might be able to tell me whether the police had spoken to him while investigating Charlie's death.

Valerie Mayhew answered the door. She tilted her head to one side when she recognized me. 'Don't you think you've done enough damage?'

Her tone took me aback. Before I could respond Heather appeared behind her in the hallway. Smaller than her friend, her cherry-red sweater replaced by a similar one in mustard yellow. Her face was pallid, her forehead creased in dismay. 'Valerie, it's all right.'

'You've heard?' I spoke directly to Heather.

She nodded. 'Damien Beswick? Just the basics. The family liaison officer we had rang me. It's already on the local radio.' Heather moved back and Valerie did, too, allowing me in. Alex came out of the living room. He glanced at me and gave a shy nod. Rowena's half-brother, I realized with a jolt. They shared Charlie's large-boned build.

'You should close the gates,' Valerie told Heather, 'before they turn up.' In the scale of things a prison suicide wouldn't bring out the press pack but the murder itself had been a huge news story and the death of the convicted killer and his claim to innocence would rekindle interest.

'I'll do it,' Alex offered and disappeared into a doorway off the hall. He was soon back and joined us in the dining room.

'He was disturbed, wasn't he?' Heather asked me. 'An addict. They said that at the time.'

'Do you think your interest, dragging it all up again, could have contributed?' Valerie jumped in.

My cheeks burnt; licks of shame. Had it? 'It's possible.' I swallowed. Damien had resisted my probing with his attempts to distract me, rambling about trivia. Was it simply too traumatic for him to recall in detail? Had facing those memories pushed him over the edge? 'I was invited to talk with him,' I said, 'by his family – his sister.' I didn't mention it was Libby who was footing the bill.

'The one who wrote the letter?' Alex asked softly. His eyes swivelled my way but never met mine.

'Yes.'

We were sat around the teak dining table. Close to Heather was a bowl of potpourri: shards and curls of wood that smelt like cedar. She was playing with it, her nails sifting through the fragments.

'What did he tell you?' Valerie asked me. 'Anything that made sense or was this change of heart something the sister dreamt up?' Her clipped words and the brusque delivery plunged me back into the headmistress's office. I resented her attitude. And felt sorry for the souls who were sent up before her on the magistrate's bench. She was much sharper than when I'd talked to her at the Civil Justice Centre. I put it down to her wanting to shield her friend from fresh troubles.

I looked at Valerie steadily then shifted my gaze to include Heather, whose face was pale and intent. 'Damien left a note,' I said, 'repeating that he was innocent.'

'No,' Heather gasped and covered her eyes with her hand. 'Why did he confess in the first place, then?' she demanded.

Alex looked at his mother, his face glum. I got the sense that he felt clumsy, miserable; a teenage boy at a loss in the emotionally fraught situation.

'I think you'd better go,' Valerie said.

'No.' Heather lifted her head, plucked at the neck of her jumper with one hand. 'His new story . . . what did he say happened?'

Valerie looked from Heather to Alex, obviously concerned for them. Heather gave her a little nod – she could take this.

I went over the basics of Damien's account: getting thrown off the bus, walking to the cottage, passing a walker coming the other way, finding the door unlocked, Charlie already dead, taking the wallet, fleeing.

When I finished Valerie's voice was sharp with scepticism: 'And had he any decent explanation as to why he admitted to the crime?'

'Only to get out of the interview situation, to tell them what he thought they wanted to hear. As you know he was an addict and he thought they'd reinstate some sort of supply once he'd owned up.'

'It beggars belief,' Valerie complained, her harsh expression emphasizing the angular planes of her cheekbones.

'I know,' I agreed. 'But I think also he realized that if he said he was guilty he wouldn't have to face a trial or go over events. It seemed the easier option in his head, at that time. Can I ask you about Nick Dryden?' I asked Heather.

'Nick Dryden?' She was surprised. 'What do you mean?'

Alex looked at his mother, startled.

'He and Charlie fell out,' I said.

'Yes. He was a horrible man. We'd no idea at first. Charming, funny, friendly, some good business ideas. It was all a front. He was a heavy drinker. And a vicious drunk.'

Alex sighed; he'd probably remember this – seven years ago, Libby had said. Had Nick Dryden been the uncle, the family friend who turned nasty? Had Alex frightening memories of the man?

'When Charlie discovered we'd lost almost everything,' Heather said, 'that Nick had been draining us dry, paying for gambling debts and fancy suits and God knows what else . . . thousands of pounds, we had to remortgage the house. There was a file this thick,' she used her hands to measure it out, 'of unpaid bills and bogus accounts: dozens of jobs where Nick had taken a deposit and never gone back. He left people a false business card. Charlie reported him. It got very nasty.'

'When did you last see him?'

'That winter. He turned up here with a baseball bat and put the windows of the Jeep in. Then he started on the conservatory. We were terrified.'

'Mum.' Alex flashed a look imploring her to stop.

'It's all right,' she said. She reached across the table and rubbed at his arm.

'What happened to Dryden?'

'I'm not sure,' she answered.

Was he missing? I'd a flash of an image: the man in a shallow grave, gone a step too far, trying to con the wrong punters. Or was he elsewhere, charming more unwitting mates into an exciting business venture, a sure-fire winner, pocketing the cash and ruining more lives? Fraudsters change their names a lot but not their way of working.

'There were rumours he'd gone to Spain,' Heather said. 'We never saw a penny. There were calls every now and then. He'd get drunk and ring up. Horrible calls – foul mouthed.'

'Recently?'

'No. They stopped.'

Because Dryden had finally got his revenge? My skin tightened. 'When?'

'It's hard to remember. Last autumn?' she said uncertainly.

'Have there been any calls since Charlie's death?'

She shook her head.

'He had a family?' I asked her.

'They moved away. Selina and the girls – to Whitby. She remarried a dentist, Tim Darville. He has his own practice. They came for Charlie's funeral.'

'Was Nick from Manchester?' I said.

'Newcastle,' Heather said, 'the Geordie accent was part of his charm.'

'Did the police speak to him about Charlie's death?'

'I don't know. They knew about him because of the trouble, but his name didn't come up again.'

'You never thought he had anything to do with it?'

'No. We hadn't seen the man for years.' But he'd continued to persecute the family with abusive calls, tormenting them for six years.

The phone rang. Alex moved to answer it but Valerie cautioned him to wait. Their answerphone kicked in followed by an eager voice, speaking rapidly. 'Mrs Carter? Jonathan Gower here, Associated Press. Can you spare a few moments to comment on today's tragedy? Are you concerned by the allegations that Damien Beswick was wrongly convicted?'

Alex stepped closer and turned down the volume. Heather sank her head in her hands.

'You could come to mine,' Valerie offered.

'I'd better go,' I told them, getting to my feet. 'If I do learn anything I'll let you know.'

'Don't you think it's best left to the proper authorities?' Valerie asked me sharply.

'I'm sure they'll be doing all they can,' I said neutrally. 'The gates?'

'I'll do it,' Alex shambled out. He could have flaunted his size, got himself in shape, built his muscles, toned his body. But he still had that slight stoop and lack of physical confidence that many boys have. And I imagined the horror of losing his dad would have completely overwhelmed any interest in normal teenage concerns and would probably continue to do so for a long time to come.

As I turned on to the main road I passed one news van, then another. The press pack was descending.

THIRTEEN

Ray had been holding the fort since I'd taken Chloe's call. Now I was returning and he would go to Laura's. My apprehension grew as I drew nearer home, my throat and shoulders tightening and a weight pressing on my chest.

Ray barely expressed any interest in where I'd been or any concern for me. We exchanged practical information about the kids before he left but the air was thick with tension and neither of us was capable of diffusing it.

Although I loathed Arndale shopping, and knew I had more than reasonable grounds to renege on my earlier promise to Maddie, the prospect of sitting gnawing my knuckles and waiting for Ray's reappearance was worse than the alternative. I tried calling Geoff Sinclair after lunch, before we left, but the phone just rang out.

We walked through the park to the local train station. The kids didn't ask to push the buggy. Jamie had become part of the furniture as far as Tom was concerned and probably something even less positive for Maddie.

The train was full of people returning from the airport, heading for connections at the main station at Piccadilly. I manoeuvred

the buggy into a space beside some luggage and stood there
while Maddie and Tom found seats in the carriage.

Piccadilly was heaving: tourists, shoppers, students and footie
fans. Flocks of teenagers in their various uniforms: Emos draped
in black with flashes of acid colour, other kids in the oversized
sportswear and gold 'bling' of the hip-hop scene and handfuls
of girls following the current fashion trend of short skirts, thick
tights, sixties backcombed hair and panda eyes. It was handy to
have the buggy so the kids could hold on and not get lost. On
our way down the ramp towards town, I saw the news billboard:
GAOL SUICIDE PLEADS INNOCENCE!

I hadn't really taken it in. That the man who'd joked and
complained and argued with me the previous day wasn't still
around; wasn't still prattling on about ghosts and drugs and cars.
Wouldn't smile again, breathe again. How unbearably desolate
he must have felt, or how fearful, to take his own life. His death
brought with it flashbacks for me to other sudden deaths that
would haunt me all my life: a man dancing aflame at a petrol
station, another bleeding to death as I held his hand, a child lost
in a house fire. I felt like crying but I didn't know who for. Then
there was the prospect of Ray's surprise love-child. And I had
two kids, a baby and shopping hell to contend with.

Both the children had spending money to get what they wanted
and we were also looking for new trousers and a winter top for
each of them. I knew we'd make more progress getting the clothes
first. Market Street was busy; hard to believe we were in the grip
of a recession. Along the central area of the pedestrianized thor-
oughfare were men with stalls selling whistles and kites and hats
with ear flaps. I heard the blues guitarist before we saw him,
shielded with an umbrella, his portable amp blasting out 'Buddy
Can You Spare A Dime'. I gave Maddie and Tom fifty pence
each to drop in his box.

H&M did a reasonable line in kid's clothing and although
everything took twice as long with buggy and baby in tow it was
pretty straightforward. Maddie got deep-red corduroy trousers
and a red and black striped fleecy top. Tom found some grey
combat pants and a hoodie with sharks on that he thought was
extremely cool.

Diane texted me asking how I was. Had she heard about

Damien and remembered that he was who I'd been to visit? Or was she waiting for news about the situation with Laura and the baby? I texted back that I was OK and would ring later.

Like most children the kids wanted to buy toys with their spending money but Manchester didn't really have a decent toyshop in the city centre. There had been a Daisy and Tom's on Deansgate but it had closed and Toys R Us was out of town and required a car and browsing on an industrial scale. However there was a German market running in St Ann's Square and we found toys and playthings in among the gingerbread and sausages and beer. Tom seized on a wooden frog that made a lifelike croak when you stroked its back with a wooden stick, and a jester's hat with bells on that he thought would be good for pirates. Maddie bought a string puppet and a wooden hula hoop. Sorted.

They were flagging by then and the walk back to the train took for ever. Thankfully Jamie didn't start crying for a feed until we were on the train. It's a quick journey, eleven minutes, but her shrieks were enough to make ears bleed. I'd have given anything for a soother but if she was used to one surely her mother would have left one in the bag. I had made up a bottle of boiled water in case she got thirsty and tried to give her some but she screwed up her face tighter and screamed even louder. We were nearing our stop and I was busy gathering our bags and avoiding eye contact with the rest of the passengers, when the crying became more muffled. A rest at last? No, just Tom, standing there with his hand over her mouth.

An hour later, calm and quiet reigned and still no sign of Ray. I got through to Geoff Sinclair. 'You've heard about Damien Beswick?' I asked.

'Yes. Not totally unexpected, though.' He sounded a little breathless, reedy.

'You think?'

He sighed. 'The lad was damaged; it didn't take an expert to see that.'

'But he was never deemed to be a vulnerable prisoner? He wasn't on suicide watch or anything?'

He grunted. 'Don't know the ins and outs of it.'

'But this changes things,' I said.

'In what way?' I heard the reserve in his tone.

Surely he could see that. 'He retracted his confession at the end; he left a note. That makes his claim to innocence much more plausible, surely? And I saw him yesterday. I used some of those techniques, the cognitive interview techniques.'

'Did you now?' He didn't try to keep the sarcasm from his voice.

'Yes. There were things that he'd not remembered before and odd things that didn't fit.' I pictured the house in darkness, the unlocked door, the car – still warm to the touch. 'I wanted to ask you: the man he passed, the one who never came forward – could it have been Nick Dryden? Charlie's ex-business partner.'

There was a pause. 'Well,' he said slowly, 'could have been. Could have been the Count of Monte Cristo, an' all.'

'Had you an alibi for Dryden? Did you speak to him?'

'No. The man had gone to ground.'

'How hard did you look, once Damien was in the frame?'

The pause went on longer. I wondered if I'd overstepped the mark.

'It wasn't deemed to be a productive use of resources. I'd say that's still the case,' he said crisply.

My mind went back to the car. Charlie driving out there, too fast. He always broke the speed limit. His one flaw, according to Libby. A new idea came to me. Could he have upset someone with his speed? An encounter with another motorist turning to road rage. The other driver following him to the cottage. An altercation, a knife on the counter. I clutched at my head trying to concentrate, grasp the whole picture.

'What if,' I said to Sinclair, 'and this is off the top of my head, Charlie had cut someone up on his way out there. He always drove too fast . . .'

'Sounds like a fairy tale.' He was dismissive. 'An imaginary traffic incident, an imaginary unknown attacker. We work with facts, we follow the evidence.'

'Who else had any motive?' I asked. 'Heather Carter, but she was with Valerie Mayhew all afternoon – unless she got Valerie to lie for her. They are friends. Valerie is . . . formidable,' I chose the word with care '. . . but she's straight as a die. I can't see her flouting the law at all – not even a parking ticket. She'd risk her whole reputation.'

'We could corroborate their accounts,' Geoff Sinclair said flatly. 'Phone records. There were calls made from the Carter house that afternoon. Third parties who could confirm that they spoke with Heather.'

'Could she have hired someone?'

'A hit man?' he scoffed. 'There were no financial irregularities, no lump sum payments to suggest anything like that, and no phone traffic between Heather Carter and persons known to the police. All these things were checked. We did our homework.' Which put me in my place?

'But maybe not on Nick Dryden,' I countered.

'I wish you luck,' he said dryly and hung up.

I was in the drive, emptying the rubbish into the wheelie bin when Ray arrived back. I saw him first, head lowered so his black curls hung over his face obscuring his expression, hands shoved in his pockets.

I froze. He sensed me and looked up, his face bleaching. He walked down the drive and I stopped breathing, felt the blood slow in my veins.

'Jamie's not Laura's,' he said quietly, his face looking tired, old.

My heart bucked with elation. I gasped with relief. Why wasn't he smiling? 'So, it was all a mix-up?' I asked him. 'She never was pregnant?'

He blinked and stretched his head back, his Adam's apple prominent against the column of his neck. 'She was,' he said and ran a hand through his hair. I glimpsed the paler skin on his wrist, the tracery of veins.

'She was?' I echoed, my voice wavering.

Ray looked down at the ground, nudged his shoe against a piece of loose concrete there.

'Ray?'

A magpie screeched high in the eucalyptus tree, then I heard the clatter of its flight.

'She has a boy,' he said. He glanced up briefly; a look of sadness shadowed his features. 'My son, Oscar.' He swung his head away and I saw his nose redden.

'Ray.' I moved in towards him, releasing my hold on the bin
bag but he shook his head. 'Later. OK?' He walked away.

I stared at the black bag at my feet, the stew of eggshells and
packaging and scraps, the rubbish of our lives blurring in my eyes.

Waiting for the computer to boot up, I picked over Ray's news,
still astounded at the very fact of it. How could we not have
heard? Manchester may be the country's second city but it's more
an urban village than an anonymous metropolis. People talk,
natter, gossip. Circles overlap. Everyone knows someone in
common; six degrees of separation becomes three. Laura only
lived a couple of miles away. How long did she think she could
keep it a secret from Ray? Why did she?

His withdrawal from me, his retreat into dealing with this on
his own rather than us tackling it together filled me with resentment. What prospect was there for us as a couple if when the
going got tough he shut me out? Yes, it was his bombshell; he'd
suddenly acquired a child he never knew about. It was huge news
to try and absorb but it affected me, too. I wanted us to share
the shock and upheaval, support each other in coping with it.
And there was the other big issue to address: if Jamie was not
Laura's child, then who was she?

Online, I began to search for Nick Dryden, setting off several
search engines and trying variations like Nicholas, too. I concentrated on any hits that linked to business. I felt sure he'd keep
operating in the field he knew. In his comfort zone. A Nick
Dryden came up twice in the north east, once linked to an insolvency hearing ten years ago. Before he'd conned the Carters.
The same old scams. Spain had been mentioned so I tried that
and found a link to a newspaper report from Benidorm in the
Costa Blanca. Nicholas Dryden was wanted by the Spanish
authorities for fraud: selling non-existent land plots and bogus
timeshares. It was believed he had left Spain and may have
returned to the UK. That was last summer. I couldn't find any
more recent reference to him online.

Was it likely, really, that after seven years Dryden would seek
out Charlie in his weekend cottage, stab him and slip away?
Revenge is best eaten cold but assuming it was Dryden something
must have been a catalyst for him to act then. Had his misfortunes

in Spain triggered fresh antagonism against the Carters? His abusive calls had stopped around the time of Charlie's murder. Was there a connection?

There was no listing on Yell.com or similar sites, and nothing on People Finder. I tried another tack: his ex-wife. A recorded announcement told me Darville's dentist surgery in Whitby was closed at weekends but there were three Darvilles listed in the local phone directory. I hit the jackpot first time.

Selina Darville was reluctant to talk to me and I had to push hard and think fast to stop her hanging up. Just the mention of Nick Dryden was obviously an unwelcome intrusion for her.

'I'm trying to trace him,' I hadn't gone into any details why, 'and all I need to know is if he's any family he would keep in touch with.'

She sighed. 'Only when he was after something.'

'Who?'

'His mother. If she's still there.'

'Where does she live?'

'I don't know if I should give out the details. It's not like you're the police or anything.'

I pleaded my case, gave her assurances and got an address. When I found a phone number to match and rang it, I learnt Mrs Kemp (she'd remarried later in life) had moved to sheltered accommodation in South Shields. The number there was busy but on my third try I got some sort of switchboard: they took my details and put me through.

I apologized to Mrs Kemp for ringing her out of the blue, and told her I wanted to get in touch with Nick Dryden. She hung up on me. Some people just don't want to help.

Frustrated, I switched my attention to the other details of the case: rereading my notes on Damien's story and attempting to draw a sketch of events. How far was it from the bus stop to the cottage? Although I'd seen pictures of the house and the village on news coverage I'd no accurate grasp of the location and the geography. Now, it seemed vital that I understood it. I should visit.

My phone went. 'Sal Kilkenny,' I answered.

There was a crackle of static, silence then faint breath sounds on the end of the line.

'Hello?' I said. 'Can you hear me?' Was it someone in trouble?

The breath came louder, not hurried – measured, ominous. The silence was deliberate. My heartbeat picked up. I held my own breath, straining to listen to see if I could discern anything about the person on the other end. It was impossible. Just the steady intake and exhalation of air. So close, so intimate it made my flesh crawl. Slamming down the receiver, I got to my feet. Paced up and down, trying to shake off the shiver of fear that had spread down my back and tugged at my guts. I dialled 1471 but of course they'd withheld the number. Was it coincidence that the call had come so soon after my attempts to track down Nick Dryden?

Ray stuck his head round the door. 'We're off to my mum's,' he said. 'Probably stay over.'

And leave me in the dark? My chest ached, I wanted him to stay. When I spoke, I tried to modulate my voice. 'And when can we talk?'

A flicker of irritation pinched at his mouth. 'Soon. Maybe tomorrow.'

'This is really hard, Ray, you shutting me out.'

'It's not like that,' he said.

'It is.'

'I need a bit of time.'

Stalemate. What was I now? The enemy? No longer the lover? Not even a friend? 'Hold me.' I hated the neediness but I wanted to be honest about my own feelings.

He hesitated. If he leaves now, I thought, without touching me, that's it. It's over. Whatever else, if he can't give me that basic reassurance then why would I want him any more?

I met his eyes, tried to brighten my face a fraction, show a glimmer of hope in the misery. He came towards me. In silence we embraced. I drank in the smell of him, salt and musk, felt the soft, brushed cotton of his shirt collar, the breadth of his chest, the way the bones in his shoulder blades fit beneath my hands.

I could have slept there.

Then he left.

FOURTEEN

Diane came over, bringing food: a Moroccan stew. Chickpeas, turnips and dates in a glossy marinade full of garlic and spices.

Diane listened out for Jamie while I got Maddie ready for bed. I have to hang on to this, I told myself. Whatever happens with Ray, I still have Maddie and Diane. Count my blessings. I imagined Chloe Beswick putting her kids to bed, numb and trying to make sense of her brother's death. And Libby, who had never been able to watch Charlie bathe Rowena, never seen him cradle his daughter or gaze at her. What of Laura, who had denied Ray the knowledge of his second son? Did she hate him? Had he broken her heart when he got entangled with me? And now that he'd found out about the child, what would she do? What would he do?

Diane was as frustrated as I was that Ray hadn't gone into the details of his meeting with Laura. 'And now he's gone running home to mummy,' she said, scathingly, 'to avoid talking.'

'To be fair,' I pointed my wine glass at her, 'that had been arranged for a while.'

'If you have to be fair . . .' she complained.

'Well, I am,' I insisted. 'Renowned for it.' The wine was talking. I'd already had several glasses and if social services had descended on me then I might well have been regarded as unfit to be in charge of a strange infant.

'She'll do her nut – Nana Tello,' I said. 'Frogmarch them down the aisle. Whisk the baby off for baptism.'

'Will he tell her?' Diane asked.

'Maybe not yet.' The more I considered it the more it rankled. 'If he has – before even talking to me properly, well . . .'

Diane's look was knowing. 'You'll do what exactly?'

I sighed. 'I don't know.'

'And what about Jamie?'

'Ditto. As far as the kids are concerned, she's overstayed her welcome. I do realize I can't let it drift on indefinitely – it'll make it impossible for me to work apart from anything else – but I'm not prepared to pick up the phone just yet.' Day six now. I tried to imagine making that call, some child protection worker on the phone listening to me try to justify why I had waited so long to report an abandoned infant. A social worker turning up in a car, taking Jamie. And perhaps the mystery of who that little girl was never answered.

'I can't believe her mother's not rung,' I said. 'Not a word. She must be thinking about her, worried sick about her.'

'Yeah.' Diane stuck a bowl of grapes in front of me.

'About work,' I said, 'if I get really stuck . . .'

She groaned and dropped her head in her hands.

'Only if I can't find anyone else,' I rushed to say.

'It was a one-off,' she complained. 'That's what you said. Anyway, I'm away Monday and Tuesday.' She grinned with relief.

'Where?'

'Dublin. New gallery have given me a room for the glass.' Before her project on Cuba, Diane had spent time with a glass blower and out of that had created an installation. She used thousands of pieces of smooth, coloured glass to make a pathway and a 'curtain' that the viewer walked through. The resulting sound, first the crinkle and crunch of the path, then the resulting chiming of the curtain and the way light spangled from the suspended globes and icicles, was wonderful. We'd gone to the preview at the Lowry in Salford. Most critics had raved but one influential commentator had been less appreciative – 'a tacky fly-curtain that will appeal to lovers of whimsy and the knick-knack brigade'.

'He can sit on it and swivel,' Diane had muttered darkly at the time. But she had complete faith in her work and its value. I envied her that self-belief, that confidence.

Diane listened while I talked about Damien Beswick, and where that left my enquiry. I admitted to her that I wished I'd given him a little more hope at that last meeting.

'Would that have been misleading?'

'Yes, I suppose. At the time I was still so unsure.'

'Hindsight's a bugger,' she said succinctly. 'But now you believe him?'

'I'd be a fool not to – his dying message to the world,' I said. 'It's such a waste; he wasn't much more than a kid.'

'What about the other man's family, the Carters – they must be all over the place?'

'They are. And the girlfriend, the one who hired me. Going through all that and then finding that everything they've been told, everything they believed about that day is suddenly meaningless. It must feel like it's happening all over again.'

'Mummy.' Maddie stood in the doorway, her wrists and ankles sticking out of her pyjamas, shoulders hunched. Her face was white. 'I had a scary dream.'

'Come on.' I got to my feet and went to her. 'Let's get you back to bed.'

'I'll get going,' Diane said. 'See myself out.'

'Have fun in Dublin.'

'I will, and let me know . . . anything . . . everything.'

'Know what?' Maddie yawned as we went upstairs.

'Oh, nothing special. So what was this dream?' She didn't need to hear about any of the uncertainty swilling round in my life. Not until things were clearer and I was surer where we were heading. If Ray and I were over. And what would happen to Maddie and me.

I lay awake most of that night, any chance of sleep ambushed by Jamie, who woke each time I drifted off. My mind was chewing over my worries. I wasn't the only person to miss signs of Damien's fragility but I longed to make reparation. Eventually I persuaded myself that the best thing I could do for Chloe, and in Damien's memory, was to actively support her attempts to clear his name. By extension anything I could find that helped the police catch the real culprit would also help Libby and the Carters.

I'm the sort of person who copes with anxiety by doing something. Problem solving. If I could focus on my investigation, work hard, it would help and give me the hope that I could achieve results and make things better. With that in mind, I set out to make good use of Sunday by combining business and pleasure. I loaded the car with baby supplies, packed Maddie and Jamie in and drove out to Thornsby to visit the site where Charlie had lost his life. I'd no expectation of entering the property – presumably it would have been sold on, the floor ripped up and replaced or professionally cleaned. There might be people living there, or perhaps it was still a holiday home for someone. Would they know the history? Would any of them get a funny feeling about the house, sense a cold spot near the door or a peculiar anxiety in the dark?

I remembered Damien's comment about the ghost in the prison. John Ellis, the hangman who'd slit his own throat. Was Damien with him now? A shadow swinging on a creaking rope in the dark end of the night. Another lost soul.

'Where are we going?' Maddie piped up, stopping my stupid fancies. Blame it on lack of sleep.

'For a walk in the country.'

'Will we see lambs?'

'I think it's a bit late for lambs, they're born in the spring. But there's a children's farm.'

'What, with children in?!' She was astounded and then saw the joke. We both laughed.

'For children. We'll walk a bit then go to the farm. It might be feeding time.'

In the bottom of the valley, where Damien got off the bus, the road ran parallel to the river. We drove past the service station on the left and the pub advertising home-cooked food. From there I could see beyond the turn off to the bus shelter on the opposite side of the road, where Damien had been chucked off. I turned right at that junction to take the hill up to the cottage. The hamlet was pretty – maybe two dozen properties in all, clinging to the valley sides. Half of them looked to have grown out of the land, built low to the ground, the stone dark and weathered with age, the windows tiny – no doubt to avoid the punitive window taxes at the time. Somewhere like this must have been a working village, digging clay or lead or quarrying. The newer houses were bigger in scale: the same limestone but raw, glowing pale grey. They boasted picture windows, veluxes on the roofs and off-road parking.

I stopped my car partway up the hill, behind a vehicle on the left before the bend where the road twisted to the right. This was where Damien had passed two stationary cars and cased them for valuables. A Mondeo and a Volvo. The car in front of me now was a Volvo. I felt the hair rise on the back of my neck. It could be the same one. I used my camcorder to capture a shot of it and took in the locale as well.

'What are you filming?' Maddie smelt a rat.

'This and that. We'll take some of you at the farm, too.'

Jamie was awake but content and kicked her legs in excitement as I fastened her seat into the buggy chassis. The previous day's fog had lifted and we had mellow autumn sunshine. Out here there was much more birdsong, the twittering of wrens and tits and finches pierced by the raucous calls of rooks patrolling two sycamores at the end of one of the gardens.

Damien had tried the cars, looked to see if there was anything worth stealing, then crossed over. I retraced his steps. As he rounded the corner he met a man coming down the hill. Pushing the buggy up the gradient, I tried to imagine the lane at night. There were some street lights, so it wouldn't have been in complete darkness. The man had been heading down the hill. Where to? The man had crossed the road after he passed Damien, which was the wrong direction for the pub and the service station. Was he heading for one of the houses on that side of the road, or one of the cars? Or the bus stop?

If he lived here, how come he hadn't been identified by the police? All the houses would have been visited, people asked to help. Damien had heard a car start as he approached the cottage. He'd frozen, listening in case it came his way but it had gone off down the hill. Driven by that man? I should have asked him if both cars had still been there when he fled down the hill after finding Charlie's body, or had either of them gone? Too late, now. I'd never know.

The road straightened out again and there was the driveway on the right, at an incline and at the top, the side door and window of the cottage. It had been sited so the front, the longer aspect looked out across the valley to the hills on the other side of the road. There was no car around, no sign of anyone about. The place did look lived in; there were some pots of cyclamens beside the door. A sign at the bottom of the drive read To Let and gave a local agency phone number.

I pulled the buggy halfway up the drive then put the brake on and told Maddie to wait there a moment.

'Why?'

'I just want a quick look up here. I'll only be a minute.'

'Why, though? 'Cos it's for rent? Are we moving?'

How does she do that, I thought? Pick up on undercurrents, on anxieties of mine, hone in on them. 'No, it's just a work thing. Now wait there.'

I filmed the approach and walked up the short drive to where it levelled out some four yards from the building. That fit with Damien's description of the car parked just by the door. He'd come outside, feeling sick and stopped by the car. He'd heard the ticking, felt the warmth of the bonnet. The only explanation for that was that the car had been used recently. So Charlie had not been here very long when his attacker struck.

The man Damien passed – Nick Dryden or whoever – was perhaps waiting for Charlie. Charlie gets back, opens the cottage, the man kills Charlie, walks down the hill to his own car and drives away, narrowly missing being interrupted or caught red-handed by Damien looking for easy pickings.

Around the front of the house was a patio and seating area by large centrally placed French doors. There might have been barn doors there once. Gauzy curtains obscured any glimpses of the interior. The view was lovely, immediately below the road dipped in and out of sight, as did the river, and beyond the hills climbed up to meet the sky. The hillsides were stitched with dry stone walls and farm buildings dotted here and there. I could hear sheep bleating from afar. It reminded me of Geoff Sinclair's place.

'Can I help you?'

I started, cold sweat prickling under my arms as a man appeared from the far end of the house. His face was wary, he was middle-aged, casually dressed and held a pair of hedging shears in one hand.

'I wanted to have a look at the cottage,' I fudged my answer.

He looked at my camcorder. 'I see. You a reporter?'

'Mummy?' Maddie piped up, out of sight.

'Wait there a minute.'

'I am!' She was getting fed up.

He looked confused. I moved towards the road, where I could see the children, inviting the man to follow. 'I'm investigating the conviction of Damien Beswick.' I waited for recognition. And got it: a small nod. 'Are you local?' I asked.

'Just down the road,' he gestured. 'I keep an eye on the place. You're not with the police?'

'Private, working for the family.' After a fashion. I passed him my card. 'The Volvo – is that yours?'

'Yes, why?' He frowned.

'You always park it there?'

'Yes,' he said.

'It was there, the night of the incident?' I chose the blander word.

'I already told the police,' he said.

'Do you remember another car, parked next to yours? A Mondeo?'

'No, people come and go. I can't see the road from my study.'

'Do any of your neighbours own a Mondeo?'

'No.' He shook his head.

'Can we go now?' Maddie yelled.

'Just coming.' I thought about the man coming down the hill. 'Do you get people hill-walking up here?'

'It's a popular spot,' he acknowledged.

'Are there footpaths up that way?' I signalled up the hill.

'No, that's private land this side, no access. All the trails are across the other side of the valley.' He jerked his head towards the view I'd admired.

So whoever Damien had passed had not been out fell-walking.

'They thought it was the girlfriend,' he said. 'Maybe they were right all along.'

'I don't think so,' I told him.

After all, she was the one who'd hired me in the first place.

When I studied the Land Ranger map I'd bought at the service station in the valley, I could see that there weren't any properties higher up the hill than Charlie's cottage: it was on the very edge of the hamlet. The residential area was very compact; perhaps there were by-laws to prevent development outside the village centre.

While at the service station, I'd also made a point of looking for CCTV cameras. There was one covering the forecourt and the shop, and another facing the exit and the road towards Sheffield and the bus shelter where Damien had got high before looking for something to steal. The police must have examined the tapes from these: it was standard procedure nowadays. So what had they found?

Maddie hung over the farm gates, cooing at various animals in turn from kid goats to Vietnamese pot bellied pigs, and Jamie stared at everything with fascinated incomprehension.

My thoughts returned to Charlie's death. In particular to the car, cooling outside his house. The car had been driven recently. Or could the engine have been going for some other reason? Some DIY task of Charlie's? Pumping up an airbed, or shining headlights on some job? Jump leads? Had someone broken down, or pretended to? Lured Charlie to give them a hand? *Always helping people out*, Libby had said, *nothing too much trouble*. Then what? My mind stalled. The door had been unlocked, the house in gloom. There was no sign of a break-in.

I kept returning to the conclusion that the murderer must have struck as soon as Charlie reached the cottage. Charlie had opened up but hadn't had time to turn the lights on, when he was attacked. Or, as Sinclair suggested, the killer had switched the lights off before shutting the door and hiding the dreadful crime. All this just minutes before Damien tried the door.

It was time to feed one of the calves. A volunteer asked who would like to have a go. Maddie's arm shot up and she gave a little jump. She went second, after a boy who giggled all the way through. The brown calf smelt of warm hair and hay and milk. Its limpid eyes, fuzzy pink nose and big teeth entranced the children. Maddie stuck the teat in its mouth and clutched the bottle with both hands as the animal tugged at it. This triggered some recognition in Jamie, who began to mewl. After the train fiasco, I was better prepared and warmed her feed with boiled water from a flask.

While Maddie continued to help feed the calf and advise those children coming after her on technique, I pulled the buggy round to the edge of a stall where a huge sow lay panting on the straw, and I punched in Geoff Sinclair's number.

'Can I come and see you again?' I asked him. 'I'd really appreciate it. Today, if possible.'

'I'm going to be out,' he said.

'When you get back then – whenever's convenient.'

There was a long pause. He was going to turn me away. I needed to talk to him; I needed information only the police would have. I stared at the sow, her belly shuddering with her breaths, her mucky trotters and large snout.

'After four,' he consented. I let out my breath.

I sat with Jamie by the duck pond. She studied my face as she fed, her eyes swinging from mine to my mouth and back again. What was she thinking? Where was her mother this soft, Sunday afternoon? I smiled at Jamie and she smiled back, losing her grip on the teat momentarily. She fed swiftly and when I raised her to wind her, one of her hands gripped my ear.

'You're a lovely girl,' I told her and she gave a ripe burp in reply.

There was no sign of Ray or Tom when we got home. Abi Dobson was free to babysit and came over in time for me to drive out to Geoff Sinclair's for four. I was tired before I set out; I'd been tired all day and had to open the car window to let the cold air refresh my senses and counteract the fatigue.

He took an age to open the door, making me think that rather than bother a sick man, the sooner I could talk to someone else involved with the police case the better. At least I hoped so. Police officers come in all shapes and sizes, from the nit-picking and officious to the generous and cooperative. Some resent private investigators; others hope to make a second career in that line. Luck of the draw.

Sinclair didn't offer me tea this time, just a seat. I looked out to where the sun was blazing over the moorland, washing the shreds of cloud with vermillion and cherry and for a split second wondered about somewhere like this for Maddie and me if we had to move, then dismissed it instantly as a passing folly. Neither of us would cope with the isolation, the distance from facilities, the need to make an effort with all the locals. Maddie would miss school and all her friends. And I'd miss mine. Working would be harder as most of my jobs are in the city; I'd spend half my life in the car.

I laid out my thoughts to Geoff Sinclair: 'If we accept that Damien told me the truth, as far as he could remember, then it suggests that Charlie was attacked soon after he reached the cottage, and shortly before Damien found him. The lights were off and the door unlocked. And Charlie's car was still warm when Damien came out of the cottage.'

Sinclair frowned at that.

'Damien felt ill,' I elaborated. 'He went to steady himself on the car. The metal was hot.'

Sinclair shrugged. 'A shock like that, the nausea, makes you sweat, that's all.'

'But he didn't just feel it, he heard it, too: the clicking of the bodywork cooling. It only came back to him when we talked. And it is such a specific, bizarre detail I'm certain it's a genuine memory. That time of year, it would take, what, ten minutes to cool off? Did you have an estimate for the time of death?'

He made a sound, an exasperated snort. 'I really don't think it's my place—'

'Please, if you can still remember?' It was a challenge of sorts as well as a plea. I reckoned he would pride himself on knowing the details of his last case. Probably older ones, too. He struck me as a conscientious man.

He was quiet for a moment, then: 'The pathologist estimated that Charlie died sometime in the four hours preceding discovery by Libby Hill at six, though time of death is only ever an approximation. We had the last sighting from Heather Carter and Valerie Mayhew at four fifteen. It would take a further fifteen to twenty minutes to reach the cottage depending on the traffic. So that gave us a time frame of an hour and a half, between four thirty and six.'

'Damien got there at four forty. He just missed the killer.'

'Or he was the killer,' Sinclair said. Wasn't he convinced by Damien's last words?

'You don't believe the suicide note?'

He shrugged and gave me a baleful look.

'Damien passed two parked cars going up the hill to the

cottage,' I persisted. 'He passed a man who was coming down, then he heard an engine start soon after. One of the cars, a Volvo, belongs to a resident. The other was a Mondeo; no one in the street owns one.'

There was a subtle shift in Sinclair's expression, a flare of interest in his bright blue eyes. Hard to read. Did he think I was on to something? 'I think the man Damien passed got in that car and drove away,' I said. 'There aren't any houses further up; there are no paths or tourist attractions. Where had he been? I think that was the killer and it could have been Nick Dryden. What about CCTV?' I said. 'The cameras at the service station on the main road, those might show Charlie's car, if anyone was following him, or anyone driving away from the village around then.'

'Wasn't working,' he said flatly.

'What?!'

'Broken. The one that covers the shop was the only one working. We didn't get anything from it.'

'Oh, for pity's sake.' The one thing that might have given credence to my theories and it didn't exist.

'Did you speak to Nick Dryden?' Sinclair asked me.

'Not yet.' I recalled the silent call, the threat of it. 'Last summer he was wanted for fraud by the Spanish authorities. He disappeared. He's still on the run. He could be back here. Heather says he continued to make abusive calls. But there haven't been any since Charlie's death.'

'Maybe the man has a shred of decency. Look, you're pointing the finger at Nick Dryden. Last time you thought it could have been road rage,' Sinclair pointed out. Another of my wild speculations that had gone belly up. 'But Damien Beswick is still the best fit for the evidence.'

Resentment burst inside me: I was tired and getting hungry and I still had to drive home and sit up half the night with an abandoned baby *and* find out if I still had a lover. And Sinclair thought I was useless.

'You don't seem very interested in finding out who did kill Charlie Carter,' I said sharply, 'or are you clinging to the original conviction?'

His round eyes glittered with anger and when he spoke his

words were tight. 'You know nothing about me but I'll tell you this: Damien Beswick was dealt with above board and by the book. He confessed to a crime and all the evidence we recovered supported that confession. If justice has not been done, he bears the responsibility. No one else.' His gaunt face trembled as he finished.

'I'm sorry,' I said, 'I didn't intend to offend you but that lad deserves to have his name cleared and the real killer should be found and tried. I'm not making things up, I'm just trying to find an explanation for new evidence. I need to pass this information on to the police; someone has to take it seriously.'

There was a pause. 'I'll make a couple of calls,' he said. 'Get you a name.'

'Thanks.'

Our parting was stiff, still taut with anger on both sides. I understood it must have been hard for him, seeing the case he'd worked so hard on crumble, have me spouting my pet theories. It would be hard for the other officers and those who would review their work. A job well done gone rancid.

FIFTEEN

'I'm sorry,' Ray said. 'I couldn't talk; I was still trying to take it in. Still am.'

'Did you tell your mother?'

'God, no!'

Small mercy. We were in the kitchen, the favoured venue for most of our family crises. The table was between us. It was getting late.

'So what did Laura say?' I felt shivery, raw, drained.

'She doesn't want me involved.' He was stung, his face drawn. 'She doesn't want my help or any maintenance, nothing.'

Some men might be relieved. But Ray? 'What do you want?' I asked quietly.

He clenched his jaw, swallowed. I looked down and saw him press his fingertips hard against the surface of the table, his nails whitening. 'I want to know him,' he said. 'I want Tom to know him.'

'Did you tell her that?'

Outside a fierce wind had blown in from the west, buffeting the trees and roaring down our chimneys.

'She's not interested.'

'Maybe in time—'

'I'm not even on the birth certificate.' He spoke quickly.

I tried to imagine their discussion. Recalled Laura as self-contained, quiet; biding her time. Amenable but no pushover. 'Was she angry, or upset?'

'Not particularly,' he said dismissively.

'Or not showing it? She might be doing this to punish you. You dropped out of her life just as she finds she's having your baby. You dropped her like a stone, Ray.'

He glowered at me, his lips pressed tight together.

'All I'm saying,' I went on, 'is that she must be hurt. It's natural she never wants to see you again. You had been happy together,' I reminded him, though it made my throat ache.

'You think she's right?' he demanded, his temper rising.

'Not about the baby. But I understand why she's taking this tack. You need some advice – legal advice,' I said.

'What's the point? It's all stacked in her favour. You see it all the time, don't you? Fathers for justice, whatever – and those guys were married.'

'So you do nothing? Roll over and let her decide? You say you want to be part of Oscar's life, so fight for it.'

Ray sighed and put his hand to his head.

'I know some lawyers,' I pointed out, 'I can ask around.' Relief was seeping through me now I knew the facts of the situation. Ray and Laura had not played out the great romantic reunion. She didn't want him. Did he still want me?

'Did you see him – Oscar?'

'Yep.' He stood swiftly, overcome by emotion. I rose, too, wanting to console him, wanting him to comfort me. He cleared his throat. 'I'm going up, I'm knackered.' He turned away. 'Night.'

My eyes pricked, my stomach contracted. I needed his touch. Physical confirmation that things were still good between us. I stewed on this for quarter of an hour and then went to his room.

He might not want sex, that was fine: just to lie together would be enough. I went in and crossed to his bed. He was fast asleep. I'd like to say I looked on him with fond sympathy and left him to rest but in truth I stalked out of there aflame with fury, and before I gave in to the impulse to smash something over his pretty black curls.

Monday morning Ray stayed in bed with a temperature and aches and pains. After I'd taken the kids to school I dialled Abi Dobson.

'Tell me you're not busy,' I said.

'Your friend not back?' she asked.

'No, they want to keep her in a bit longer,' I lied, feeling heat in my face.

'Well, I'm not busy. Give me ten minutes.'

'You're a lifesaver,' I said.

'It's great for me,' she replied, 'some extra cash.'

'I'll bring her round to yours,' I said. 'I've some calls to make there and then I need to go to the supermarket. Not sure how long I'll need.'

'It doesn't matter, I've nothing else on today.'

I caught Monica Meehan, Damien's lawyer, on the phone before she left for court. When I'd explained why I wanted to see her, she hummed and hawed over her diary, finally squeezing me in early on Friday morning. She also cautioned me that there would be a long way to go before anyone could start talking about quashing the conviction. And the possibility of reopening the investigation would be up to the CPS.

I rang Libby. 'How are you bearing up?'

'OK,' she replied. 'Apart from some jerk from the tabloids who had fun shouting through the letter box.'

'When was this?'

'Yesterday. He gave up after a few hours.' The sarcastic edge disappeared from her voice as she added: 'He said the police will want to interview me again. Just the thought of that—'

'They have no evidence against you,' I reminded her. 'They hadn't back then and they still don't. You were close to Charlie and you found him. That's why they had to consider you.'

'I know. It was horrible, though. It's so frightening to be in that situation, I don't think people have any idea. It's really scary.' There was a tremor in her voice. I couldn't help but think of Damien and how he'd chosen to lie, to sentence himself to time behind bars rather than endure the interrogation.

'He was just trying to get a reaction from you – something to quote in the paper,' I said.

'Bloody hyenas,' she complained.

'Have they been back?' I checked.

'No. But I'm lying low for now. So, is there any news?'

'Things aren't going to move quickly,' I told her and outlined what I was doing.

'Should I do anything?' she asked. 'Write to the police and demand they reopen the investigation or whatever?'

'Good idea. The more pressure there is coming at them the more likely they'll have to be seen to be doing something. Address it to the chief constable.'

'Right. I'll do that.'

'But don't get your hopes up,' I warned her.

'You're saying all I might end up with is that they charged the wrong man.'

'I hope it's more than that but these things can take years. And there's a limit to what I can do. The ball needs to be back in the police's court. They have jurisdiction. They have the authority.'

After I'd sorted my mail and email messages, I locked the office and went upstairs. Abi and Jamie were in the living room. Jamie was dozing and Abi was watching TV.

'I'm off to the supermarket now,' I said, 'then I might try and do a bit more work if that's OK.'

'Cool.'

'Do you want anything bringing?'

Abi grinned. 'Ice cream – chocolate fudge.'

'You got it.'

As I opened the car door, there was a blur of movement beside me. A flapping of material. Black wings obscuring my vision. Hands grabbed my wrists, forced them behind my back, gripping them both in one large fist, strong as a vice. Acid rose in my throat and my heart thumped with fear.

'Get in,' a voice hissed, hot breath in my ear.

I resisted, digging my heels into the ground, locking my knees, but the man held on to my wrists and used his other hand to push my head down and shove me forward. I sprawled across the front seats, bruising my chin on the handbrake. My feet were still outside the car and I kept kicking out, hoping to connect with his shin or kneecap. He leant in after me and yanked my hands up; pain tore across my shoulders.

'Get in,' he repeated. Kicking at my shoes, pushing my legs out of the way with his foot, thrusting me up against the passenger door. He followed me inside the car and slammed the door shut.

I tried to kick out but there was no room for manoeuvre. My knees were in the footwell, legs bent, my feet crushed against the gearstick. He belted me across the head with his free hand. The blow rang in my temples, sickening. Then he pressed my head down against the far edge of the passenger seat. He was very strong. The hard plastic moulding of the door bit into the right side of my jaw.

'You've been looking for me.' A gravelly voice, a Geordie lilt. 'You've been harassing my mother.'

Nick Dryden. 'No.' I fought to sound calm, my voice was muffled, distorted as my mouth was pushed out of shape, pressed against the fabric weave of the seat. 'I just wanted to contact you.'

'Who for?' he said.

'What?'

'Who are yous working for?'

I wasn't going to tell him. It seemed like a peculiar question, anyway. 'Talk,' he demanded. 'Who are yous working for?'

'It's about Charlie Carter,' I managed. It was hard to talk with the weight on my head.

'He's dead, isn't he?' he said brutally. 'The bloke 'as did it topped hisself?' Any charm Dryden might have had was definitely switched off.

'He didn't do it,' I said thickly.

'So . . .?' He barked a laugh as though he'd just got a joke. Then again. 'So that's what this is about?'

I thought about raising a foot, trying to hit the horn, draw attention and get help, but I would have to swing round and raise my knee from the floor to get any leverage. Impossible. If he relaxed his grip on my wrists, I could fling the passenger door open and scramble out on to the pavement. But while he held me so tight, I couldn't do anything. I do self-defence classes but we'd never learnt any moves that I could use in this particular situation.

'You think I'm mixed up in that? You stupid little bitch.'

At least he didn't come in the Dobsons' house, I thought. The image of him menacing Jamie or Abi threatened to unseat me. Tears scorched my eyes. I squeezed them back, focused on my rage at the man, my anger.

'Aren't you?' I asked him. 'You'd been friends and then you ripped him off, practically ruined him.'

'Bastards,' he swore, 'him and his bloody wife. Stood by while my family was kicked out on the streets, destitute. Totally ruthless they were and she was worse than him. Fair-weather friends they were,' he banged on, 'they never give us a chance.'

But Selina had attended Charlie's funeral, she had kept in touch with the Carters, obviously siding with them in the dispute with her ex-husband. Dryden had his own world view, styled to suit himself. A narcissist. He saw himself as the victim in all this. Probably the only way he could live with himself.

'You stole from the business, you smashed up their car, made abusive calls.'

'Doesn't mean I swung for the bloke.'

'You expect me to believe you?'

The sudden release of my wrists and my head was unexpected. I scuttled round, my nerves chattering, expecting a fresh blow.

Dryden, big-boned, florid, corned-beef complexion, was yanking his shirt from his jeans. I froze. Oh, God – he was going to rape me. Saliva flooded my mouth and I wanted to gag. I began to twist, aiming to get the door handle, when he spoke.

'Look.' He pulled up his shirt to reveal a pasty, swollen belly and, running up from his navel, a rope-like scar, silvery and pink. 'Double bypass. Bonfire night, last year.' He beamed at me, a deranged, triumphant light in his eyes. 'Read all about Charlie's murder when I was in the hospital.'

Bonfire night was three days before the murder.

He barked with laughter again, tugged his shirt down and drew the sides of his long black coat around him. Then he lunged back at me, gripping my chin in one meaty hand. As he spoke spittle landed on my face and I could smell his breath: stale fags, the pee-like scent of whisky and something dead. I could see the nicotine stains in the grooves on his long yellow teeth. 'It's nowt to do with me, petal, and if you ever,' he squeezed my jaw tighter, 'ever, come sniffing after me or bother my mother again, I'll carve you up. And,' he nodded towards the house, 'that little bairn an' all.' He let go. My jaw burned. I was trembling, inside and out, unable to control the shakes.

He opened the door and put one foot down on the road. 'I wasn't here.' He leant back towards me, his voice whispery now. 'You never saw us.'

He swivelled round and the car bounced at the shift in weight as he stepped out. He slammed the door and walked round to the back of the car. My breath came in jagged gasps, terror and relief, as I followed his progress in the rear-view mirror.

He took a few steps away, still on the road, then wheeled back towards my car. His hand pulled something from his coat pocket: a short metal bar. He raised his arm and slammed the weight against the back windscreen. I flinched as the glass fractured into a thousand pixels and fell, a great wash of crashing, crystal sound.

Then he strode off, his coat flapping, and rounded the corner.

Even then, no one came; just another noise in the symphony of the city.

I sat for long enough, waiting for my heart to steady, for the sheen of sweat on my skin to cool. A sob broke in my mouth, then another. I let them come, releasing the fear and distress, the fury at my impotence, my powerlessness and the vicious bastard's power to hurt me.

When the crying was done I wiped my face, blew my nose and eased over into the driver's seat.

My keys were in the footwell there, where I had dropped them. Picking them up, I wondered who I could call. Not Ray. And Diane was still in Dublin. I looked back at the rear windscreen, the bits of glass fringing the hole like some entrance to an ice cave. She'd appreciate it. There was no one to call.

'Fine,' I said aloud, my voice husky with tears. 'Just absolutely fucking fine.'

Then I started the car, took it to have the rear windscreen repaired and went shopping. The world still turned; we still had to eat.

I felt jaded, numb, indifferent even. It was a mask, I think, born of shock, something to get me through the aftermath of being so frightened. And I had to be strong, keep functioning, because there was no one else. I was on my own.

SIXTEEN

While I put the shopping away, I thought about Dryden. He'd left Spain to escape the fraud charges there, and presumably thought I was tracing him for the Spanish authorities or his creditors. His alibi, if it could be proven, was a strong one. And taken with his demeanour, the way he'd sought me out and threatened me meant I no longer considered him a credible suspect. If he was a killer, he'd never have crawled back out of the woodwork like that. He'd have stayed hidden, protected himself.

With Damien gone, and Dryden ruled out, there was no one else who looked guilty. The person most likely to – Heather Carter – had a sound alibi backed up by her respected friend and by third parties.

So, if it wasn't someone who knew Charlie could it have been an act of random violence? My mind returned again to the possibility of it being a road rage incident. Valerie said they'd tailed Charlie's car as far as the turn off, then retraced their route home. Might Valerie have seen any bad driving, any trouble between Charlie and other motorists? Surely she would have said as much when notified of his death. Had she seen anyone else following Charlie's car? Or had Heather? I was reluctant to intrude on the Carters again but plucked up the courage to try Valerie Mayhew. No answer. She might be at the Civil Justice Centre.

At reception, they told me which court Valerie Mayhew was sitting in. I slipped into her courtroom and her eyes flicked my way, freezing for a moment in clear displeasure when she saw who I was.

They were considering a case of non-payment of council tax. Mayhew, sitting in the centre of the panel of three, instructed the man concerned that he would be expected to pay his arrears off at a given rate. She gave him a brief lecture on the powers of the court to act if he failed to comply. The man was dismissed and there was a break between cases. Valerie Mayhew whispered something to her colleagues and they gathered their papers and left. She made her way over to where I was sitting.

I saw her pause and narrow her eyes as she made out the bruising already flaring on my jaw and cheek. Underneath my clothes I could feel a whole bunch more of them emerging.

'I hope you won't be making a habit of this,' she said crisply. 'I have work to do.'

'And I'm trying to do mine,' I said calmly. 'I won't keep you long.'

She inclined her head but didn't sit, reinforcing the impression of a strict teacher.

'It's about when you followed Charlie in the car.'

She blinked, frowning. I don't know what she'd expected me to ask but it wasn't this.

'Did you see anything happen on the way? Any near misses, any trouble between him and other motorists?'

'No,' she replied.

'You could see him all the time? Were you immediately behind him?'

'At first, then there was a car between us. Why?' she said.

'Weren't you afraid he'd recognize you, or the car?'

'A little, but it was dark. I don't suppose most of us pay attention to who's behind unless there's a problem.'

'Was there anyone following you?'

She frowned, shook her head. 'I've no idea.'

'The car that came between you – did it turn off with Charlie?'

She thought for a moment, 'No, it carried on.'

'And you never lost sight of him? You'd no problem keeping up?'

'None at all. The traffic was slow moving. I wondered if he'd noticed us. That's why I let the other vehicle in. What's all this about?'

I wasn't sure any more. Maybe Charlie had annoyed a motorist further along into his journey. Maybe there was no road rage incident and Sinclair was right. I was scrabbling for theories.

'Just background,' I smiled. The gesture hurt my cheekbone.

She didn't smile back. 'I really must get on,' she said. 'And I'd rather not be interrupted at work in future.' And with that she walked off.

Ray was still in bed. I'd put my head round his door to see if he wanted a cup of tea, figuring that an amiable approach from me might improve things between us more quickly than if I left it up to him (Ray's default mode during conflict was to sulk). He was still asleep.

Abi asked me about my face when I swapped ice cream for Jamie, and I'd told her I'd managed to collide with the back door on the hatchback when I was loading the shopping. 'I'm always doing it,' I said. 'Never learn.'

After grabbing something to eat, I fed and changed Jamie. I talked to her and watched her mimic me: trying out shapes with her mouth as I babbled on. 'What are we going to do with you?' I rubbed her tummy. 'What are we going to do?'

It was a good job Ray was out of it; otherwise he'd be back on my case, telling me it was now day seven and we needed to alert social services to the situation. The prospect made me queasy. How would they regard the week-long delay in contacting them? Might they turn the spotlight on me, my motives, examine my circumstances? I'd probably be treated with suspicion at the very least, or as a nutter. With a squirt of anxiety, acid in my stomach, I wondered if they'd question my ability to care for Maddie. Would they want to assess me as a parent? A frightening prospect. Now I was getting paranoid. Wasn't I?

The doorbell went at one o'clock. I was cautious, jittery, still shaken by the attack and so I checked through the glass before opening the door.

It was a young woman. She'd long hair, dyed an artificial crimson colour, the vivid tone contrasting with the pallor of her face. She was of slight build and wore a bright green coat with three-quarter length sleeves (a style that would make my wrists ache in the cold), black leggings and fake Ugg boots.

'A'right,' she said.

Did I know her? There was something familiar in the shape of her face, the narrow planes, sharp nose, the cast of her eyes. She snorted, shook her head and the light glanced off the sheen in her hair, she cut her eyes away and back at me. 'Leanne,' she announced. 'Yeah?'

Leanne! The hair had changed from the mousy rats tails I remember and she was a few years older, but now I knew her. The first time we met she'd been a homeless waif plaiting bracelets to make a few pounds, squatting in an abandoned warehouse. She'd been part of a case I was working on. She'd had a traumatic life in care, horribly abused by the people supposed to be looking after her. The boy I was searching for had been violated in the same way. Parties in the care homes, the young and the vulnerable easy pickings for the powerful men who got pleasure from raping children. I didn't know all that until it was almost too late. Leanne helped me out at first, then blamed me when things went wrong. I took her out for a meal and to pump for questions and she stole from me. The last time I saw her, she was in fear for her life. I watched her shoot a man dead, vengeance and damage etched on her face, and run away. She was thirteen years old, then. She probably saved my life. I'd never expected to see her again; I'd doubted she'd survive. I'd expected her to disappear into a world of addiction and dispossession. Die alone, in some squalid squat.

'Leanne,' I said, still fumbling for comprehension.

'Where is she, then?' She had a huge sports bag by her side and hoisted it over her shoulder, stepping inside. She smelt of cigarettes and fabric conditioner.

'Jamie.' Connections were sparking, fizzing and rearranging in my mind. I felt dizzy.

'Jamie?' Leanne dumped her bag in the hall and pushed the door shut. 'She's not called Jamie.' She sounded disgusted, her lip curling at the thought.

'I'd no idea what she was called,' I retorted. 'You didn't put that on the note, did you?'

'Oh, soz. It's Lola. Jamie's a boy's name.'

'Not always,' I argued.

'Jamie Oliver.' She flung back the name of the celebrity chef. She glanced around the hall, moving into the playroom. Quick, nervy, still a wild quality to her. Questions crowded my head; where to start? She turned to me, her face narrowing with suspicion. 'Where is she? You didn't put her in care?' Her eyes shimmered with anxiety and her voice shook.

'She's here.' I led Leanne into the lounge.

'Lola.' She scooped up the baby, hugged her close and kissed her head, then her cheeks, repeating her name and hugged her close again. Her own eyes closed, Lola kicked her legs, chuntered.

'Where've you been?' I asked Leanne. 'What on earth made you leave her? Why here?'

Leanne continued to cradle her daughter, swinging her hips slightly from side to side.

'What's going on?' Ray came in, still in his pyjamas.

Leanne opened her eyes. 'Cool jim-jams.' She nodded.

'Leanne,' I tried to stay on track, 'I didn't even know it was you. Why didn't you explain?' I looked over to Ray. 'Leanne, Jamie's mother.'

'Lola,' Leanne corrected. She patted the baby's bottom. 'What's she wearing?'

'Reusable nappy,' I said.

'Ugh, gross.' She curled her lip.

'Where've you been, Leanne?'

'You know her?' Ray asked me.

'She was a friend of J.B. – the guy who had Digger.' J.B., a homeless lad himself, had been a kind friend to Leanne and other homeless youngsters. He had been killed when he got too close to the paedophile ring I was investigating. I found his body.

'You kept Digger.' Leanne nodded. Then her face altered: sudden worry again. 'He all right with the baby?'

'Keeps out of the way,' I said. 'Why didn't you come in and tell me what was going on? Instead of just leaving a note. I'd no idea who the baby was, who'd left her.'

'You might have turned us down,' she said with a shrug. 'And I put my name on, anyway.'

'It was illegible,' said Ray coldly.

'Sorry,' she said, sounding anything but.

'Why leave her?' I asked.

'It's complicated,' she said.

Ray sat down in one of the armchairs; he looked horribly serious. 'So, explain,' he said.

'Go on.' I sat on the sofa.

Leanne sighed. 'I had to make myself disappear for a bit. I didn't know where I'd end up. I couldn't take her with me.'

'Why did you have to disappear?' Ray asked.

'Who's he?' Leanne complained to me. She was a teenager still, trying to play us off against each other.

'Answer the question, Leanne.'

'This bloke, he's bad news, he won't take no for an answer. He's been inside and he was coming out, expecting to play happy families.'

I heard Ray groan, dismayed at the scenario.

'He's your boyfriend?' I asked her.

'Was. For, like, five minutes. I didn't want him near her.'

My heart sank. It sounded like Leanne was still stuck in the same murky, dangerous world as when I'd last known her.

'Why me?' I asked.

She shifted Lola to the other shoulder. 'He never knew about you – wouldn't have a clue. Anyone else, he might have guessed. You helped us out before,' she said gruffly, a wash of colour in her cheeks.

'How did you know I was still here?'

'The phone call about energy suppliers?' She smirked. I'd a dim recollection, a cold call.

'You hung up on me halfway through the spiel. And you're in the Yellow Pages so I knew you were still in business. So I brought Lola here, then I kept moving.'

'Where did you go?' I asked.

'Seaside. Friggin' cold.'

'Where did you sleep?'

'Wherever.' She raised Lola up, held her by the waist and let her fly, arms extended like a little astronaut.

'Outside?' Ray clarified.

Leanne shot him a pitying look and lowered Lola.

'Won't he still be looking for you?' I was worried for her, for the baby.

'Nah. He got into a scrap on Saturday night, glassed this bloke. He's out on licence so he goes straight back in.' She smiled, lowered Lola and held her on one hip. I thought of Chloe Beswick, managing with her kids, planning her brother's funeral.

'So, where are you living?' I said.

'Been over in Leeds for a while. I'm on the list for a place; they say it could be eighteen months. I'm at a mate's, on the couch. Her bloke's fed up with us being there so I might have to find somewhere else. She been all right for you, then?'

'You don't seem to have any idea of the trouble you've caused.' Ray spoke; I could tell from his tone that he was furious.

'What trouble?' Leanne's lip curled.

'Ray,' I tried to interrupt, calm him down. I knew Leanne's apparent recklessness; her insouciance was as much a front as anything else. Lecturing her would only provoke more of the same.

'What if we'd gone to the authorities?' he demanded.

'Well, you didn't, did you?' she flung back at him.

'If it had been up to me—'

'Well, I didn't leave her with you, I left her with Sal. Wouldn't leave a bloody goldfish with someone like you.'

They were squaring up like dogs for a fight.

'And now you expect us to watch you pick up the baby and sail off, God knows where, sleeping on the streets with her.' He got to his feet.

Leanne jabbed a finger at him. 'You don't know anything about me, mate, so keep your nose out.'

'Can you look after her? Properly?' he challenged.

'Ray, please—' I tried.

'Yes, I bloody can. I left her here, didn't I, to keep her safe. She's never had to sleep on the streets, she's never gone hungry. I look after her.' She was worked up, shouting. Lola was beginning to whimper. I didn't want Leanne storming out, for the whole thing to collapse into a slanging match.

'Of course you can,' I said steadily. 'Let's just calm down. Look, you'd like a cup of tea, something to eat?'

Ray made a blurting sound. I ignored him.

'Yeah, ta.' She patted Lola again, whispering to her, turning her back on Ray.

'Ray?' I nodded to him to get out and make the tea. I thought he'd combust. 'I'd like to talk to Leanne in private. What'd you like?' I asked her. 'Beans egg, toast?'

'Yeah, ta.'

Ray gave a hollow laugh. 'You want to feed her, you make it.' He strode out of the room.

Leanne swung round, raised her eyebrows to me. 'Knobhead,' she said.

'So, how are you doing, really?' I said quietly.

'Fine.'

'Leanne,' I said gently, 'it can't have been easy—'

She sat on the floor, settled Lola on her back between her legs so the child could see her face, Leanne held the baby's feet, rubbed her thumbs against the small soles. 'It hasn't, but soon as I was expecting I got myself sorted, cleaned up.'

'You were using?' I tried to keep any censure from my voice.

'Just pills. Not now, though. Nothing since, well . . . a bit of weed. I'm not going to mess this up.' She met my eyes, a moment's direct honesty. 'You know what happened to me,' she reminded me. She paused for a fraction, the bitter history hung in the air. 'Well, I did a parenting course,' she said. 'There's this project in Leeds. It's good. I'm gonna do an access course when she's bigger. I'm going to do right by her.'

I believed her. Or at least I believed the desire behind it. Whether she'd be able to overcome the weight of her past, change the fate she had been dealt and reinvent her life was impossible to guess. 'What would you like to do?'

'Youth work,' she said, quick as a flash. 'Have to get some exams first. But the tutor says I could do it, just need to put the work in.'

'Good. I'll get that food.'

Leanne scrambled to her feet and picked up Lola. In the kitchen she strapped her in the baby seat and chattered to her while I made the meal. When I put the plate down in front of her she said, 'Ta,' and began to eat ravenously, smacking her lips and with her eyes on Lola in between.

'This place you're staying,' I asked her, 'you said it was in Leeds?'

'Chapeltown. I might move back this way but then I don't

know if they'd transfer me on the lists. Could try the housing associations.'

'And the access course?' I said.

'They'll have the same sort of thing here.'

Ray came in. He still hadn't got dressed and ignored us and began making a cup of tea.

Lola grinned and blew a raspberry. Leanne waved her fork at her.

When I thought of them leaving, Lola disappearing, it gave me a hollow ache inside. Then I had an idea. Crazy but perfect.

'You got any biscuits?' Leanne asked.

I found her some shortbread. 'We've got a room to let,' I said. 'A flat – on the top floor.'

'You are joking!' Ray exploded, slamming his teaspoon on to the counter.

'Don't think Mr Hitler there's all that keen,' Leanne smirked.

'Sal,' Ray warned, 'no way.'

'A trial run,' I said to both of them. 'A month. You'd have to pay your way,' I told Leanne, 'rent, bills.'

'Once my benefits come through,' she qualified.

'You are out of your mind,' Ray said to me. 'We decide on tenants together – you can't just unilaterally invite her like this.'

I felt my own anger rising. 'I just did.' I was truculent, even more determined to see the idea through now Ray was so riled. Why did he always have to be so po-faced about things? With our lives in such a state of flux, I didn't even know if he'd be here with me in a month's time. 'We need a tenant, she needs a room. It's a good place for a baby—'

'We have got enough going on without all this.' He gesticulated wildly at Leanne and Lola. 'You playing bloody social worker.'

'Stop overreacting!' I yelled.

'I can't talk to you when you're like this,' he threw back his head, 'and she is not moving in without my agreement.' He walked out.

Leanne exhaled noisily. 'That's a no, then?' she said.

'I don't give up that easily,' I told her. 'There are house rules, though.'

'Like agreeing who moves in?'

I started to smile, stopped as my face ached. 'No smoking for a start.'

'I never smoke in the house, it's bad for Lola. I'll just nip out now, though.' She fished rolling tobacco and papers from her pocket.

When she came back in, I took her up to the attic and gave her the tour. It's a nice flat, sloping ceilings, a view of the garden from the main room, a smaller room furnished as a bedroom across the landing, shower and WC between. Basic furnishings. Leanne settled Lola on the rug while we looked round.

'You'd have to share the kitchen, downstairs,' I explained.

She was looking out of the dormer window; she'd gone very quiet.

'No wild parties,' I said, 'no trouble, you'd have to keep it nice. You could redecorate if you want.'

She turned her head to mine, her arms crossed in front of her. 'Why would you do that? Let me stay?' Her face was serious, almost angry-looking.

'We need a lodger.'

'But me, bit of a risk, isn't it?'

'Yeah,' I admitted. 'Maybe I like the odd risk.'

She blinked and looked away, her jaw flexed; she was moved and I felt my own throat ache in response.

'You know what I did,' she said softly. It was a question as much as anything. Did it matter, would I report her, did it define her?

'Yes. And I know why.' I thought back to that night in the park, dark, drizzling. Looking for a lost boy before his captors found him. Men in the dark, fists and guns. Fear coursing through me. Bones running soft. The gunshot to my shoulder throwing me back against stone. Leanne, hiding in the gloom, firing at the man, killing him. Blood everywhere. 'We can't change the past.' In the quiet I could hear the clatter of a train in the distance. 'You're making a go of things, now.'

'Yeah. But yer man isn't too happy.'

'I'm not sure he is my man,' I said frankly.

'How's that?'

'Maybe later,' I put her off.

'Yer better off without him,' she said vehemently.

'Why's that?'

She looked incredulous. Nodded. 'Your face?'

I touched my jaw where a bruise had blossomed courtesy of Nick Dryden. 'No,' I smiled, grasping her meaning, 'it's nothing like that. That's not him.' And Ray hadn't even noticed, hadn't mentioned it. My shoulder was throbbing too and so were my shins, where Dryden had kicked at me so viciously. 'You think I'd stay with someone who was beating me up?'

'Plenty do. It's not just to wind him up, is it? To spite him? 'Cos if it is—'

'No,' I broke in. Though a teensy bit of me had enjoyed provoking that reaction. 'Maybe you deserve a break. I was on my own with Maddie, at first. It was hard. Too hard. Finding this place, sharing with Ray, it got a lot easier. He's got a little boy.' Two, I thought to myself. 'And Lola, well, she's lovely.'

Leanne grinned. 'She been sleeping?'

'Not so's you'd notice,' I muttered, Leanne-style. The prospect of an unbroken night swam into view. Oh, bliss. 'She's got a tooth,' I suddenly remembered.

'No way! Let's see.' She picked her up, started praising her.

'What do you think, then?' I asked her. 'A month's trial?' I glanced at my watch; I needed to collect Maddie and Tom.

'What about him?' she asked me.

'I'll deal with him.' I sounded more confident than I felt.

'Cool. I'll have to let the council know, could be months before they sort my benefits out.'

'That's OK. Good. And I meant it about the rules – any trouble, anything dodgy, and it's off, no second chance.'

She opened her mouth and I expected protest, injured pride, but she took stock and instead just nodded. ''Course.'

'I've got to get the kids from school. Make yourself at home. If you want a shower, there are towels in the cupboard in the bathroom downstairs. There's sheets and bedding there, too, if you want to make up the bed.'

She nodded, did that funny little blink again. 'Ta.'

As I reached the first-floor landing, Ray was there, arms folded, stern from head to toe, his eyes hot with fever and frustration. 'We have to talk about it; you can't just let her move in.'

My throat hurt. 'We need to talk about a lot of things, Ray:

us, this, Laura, Oscar.' I pulled on my jacket, aware that this time I was the one postponing time to discuss things. 'We can talk this evening, or tomorrow,' I suggested.

'So she stays tonight?' he huffed. 'She's not going to want to move once she's got her feet under the table.'

'You don't know her,' I objected.

'Do you? Know her well?'

I thought of my past with Leanne. The dreadful things she'd been through, the terrible things she'd done, things that I would not tell Ray – not now, maybe never.

'I know her enough to give her a chance. And there is no way on earth I would offer her the flat if I thought it couldn't work out. I'd never risk what we've got here.' I hoped he'd soften then, acknowledge that what we had something, something important, permanent. But he gave me nothing. 'I'd better go.'

He stood there, a sadness in his eyes now, as though we'd lost something. Maybe we had. Maybe we couldn't hold on to that first flush of passion with so many upheavals coming our way. I felt sad, too, more so as I realized I didn't have the courage to approach him. If I laid a hand on his shoulder or touched his cheek with my palm would he shy away, slap me down? I didn't have the heart to find out.

SEVENTEEN

We didn't talk that evening. Ray kept to his room and didn't even join us for tea. Leanne was introduced to Maddie and Tom and made quite an impression, teaching them some complicated hand-jive greeting and some street slang (inoffensive as far as I could tell). I spent half an hour picking bits of glass out of the back of the car. Leanne could not believe we hadn't got a working telly. She stared at me, aghast.

'I thought people your age were multi-platform,' I said.

'You what?'

'MP3, Internet, downloading movies to your phone.'

'Yeah, but you still need a telly,' she said.

'We are going to replace it, just not had chance,' I explained. She sighed.

'Sheila had one in the flat. There's an aerial socket up there. In fact, that would make sense, to get you one of your own.'

'Cool.'

It wasn't a completely altruistic move; I didn't want to be fighting Leanne over which programme to watch. I imagined our tastes would differ somewhat. And having a lodger seemed to work best when we had a degree of autonomy.

'Won't be anything fancy, mind. No plasma or 3D.'

'I made a list,' she said, 'stuff for the flat. Some of it they might give me a grant for.' She handed me the piece of paper. In the same neat capitals that had been on the note she'd printed out: CURTAINS, CHANGING MAT, COT, LAMP.

'What colour curtains?' I said.

'Something shiny would look good against that colour blue. Maybe a gold, or dark blue with some sparkle in it.'

'Ever made any?' I asked her.

'You having us on?' Her eyes sparkled with merriment.

'I've a sewing machine – you can get fabric at the market, or there's a good place in town I know. It's not hard. I'll show you.'

'OK. Give us summat to do while we're waiting for the telly,' she grumbled.

I smiled.

I'd gone into my usual practical mode after Dryden's attack: sleeves up, head down, all systems functioning. Keep calm and carry on. Driven, I'd managed to get the car repaired, do my chores and continue investigating for Libby Hill. On top of all that I'd handled Leanne's Lazarus act and found myself in a stand-off with Ray.

But just as the bruises all over my body were coming into full bloom, the colour of butter yellow, mottled with blue, reminding me of pansies, so the emotional and psychological impact of the assault was bubbling to the surface. And as soon as I stopped racing about, filling my time keeping busy busy busy, I could feel my composure splitting and fraying, tearing apart.

The nervy unease in my stomach as I showered and got ready for bed was the start of it. And a cup of warm milk and honey did nothing to lay it to rest.

Now Leanne was here and Lola would be sleeping – or not – upstairs in the flat with her, I should have been able to immerse myself in a deep and healing sleep. I started out OK. My eyes grainy and tired, the bed blissfully comfy once I'd found a way to lie without putting pressure on my sore bits. No need to listen for the sound of a baby breathing or panic if it was too quiet.

I closed my eyes and tried to empty my mind: banishing Charlie Carter and Damien Beswick, Ray and Laura and their baby Oscar. I struggled to fill the space with fantasies. Holiday dreams, perhaps. When that failed and scenarios started playing out where Ray and Tom and Digger moved away, leaving Maddie and I weeping on the threshold, I resorted to doing multiplication: working out how much rent to charge Leanne and what that would be per month, per year. The dullness of that succeeded, enabling me to sleep but then the dream came.

I was in the garden, by the pond. It was summer, high summer and uncommonly warm. I was on the sun lounger and Lola was in my lap. She was happy, gurgling. A shadow fell across us. I looked up, dazzled by the sun and saw the silhouette of a man. Dread shot through me. Nick Dryden was there. He was shouting and as he did he tore at his shirt, pulling it apart. The scar on his stomach, ridged and ropey, began to open, peeling apart like a zip, and blood poured out. Dark red and sticky, glistening in the sun. I was screaming, trying to get up from the lounger but my legs had no power in them: my bones had turned to water.

Then I was standing in the house and he was breaking all the windows, the sheets of glass crazing then collapsing like a crash of ice cubes. Over and over. Leanne came in through one of the broken windows; she had a gun in her hand.

'Get out!' I screamed to her, 'He's here.'

She didn't move. She was staring at me, her face urgent, deadly serious. She just said, 'Where's the baby?'

I had lost the baby. I couldn't find the baby. I started hunting under the cushions, behind the settee. The television was on the floor. There was blood on the carpet. There was something under the television. I saw a small hand, tiny fingernails, like translucent shells. I began to cry. I had killed the baby.

'I'm sorry.' I turned, gulping. Leanne had gone. But Valerie Mayhew was there, with her straight, silvery hair, bright eyes, her smartly tailored suit.

She held the gun now. 'That's your baby,' she said. 'You have to go to the police.' She was shaking her head, severely disappointed in me.

It was Maddie. I'd killed Maddie. My eyes filled with tears as the enormity of what I'd done, that dreadful, dreadful mistake tumbled through me. I'd destroyed everything: my lovely precious girl dead, Ray gone and Tom, too. Maddie was dead.

I reared awake, slick with sweat, my heart aching, bile in my throat. It took me a few moments to really believe that it had only been a dream. I felt so sullied by it, so tainted, that I needed proof, to reorientate myself in the here and now. To banish the monsters.

The children were there: safe, asleep. The night light glowing, the toys and posters and bedding familiar. I watched them for a while. If I could have wept, it might have helped; I craved release but I couldn't let go. The fear and the tension clotted in my chest, gripping my throat. As if I had swallowed a rock.

Downstairs I found the arnica that we give the kids for upsets and minor injuries. Something I should have taken straight after I'd been hurt. I swallowed a pill. Digger, sleeping under the kitchen table, opened one eye, then decided it wasn't worth his while to do more than that and closed it again. His tail twitched. Dreaming already. Swap you, I thought. Rabbits and tree trunks for dead babies and guns.

I'm not completely lacking in self-awareness, just a bit slow getting there at times. A few bouts of counselling in the wake of other traumas meant I recognized what my body or my psyche was telling me to do: to slow down, to care for myself and take some space to recuperate. But what about work, was my knee-jerk reaction. It'll keep, I reminded myself. Take a day, one day. Nothing is going to change significantly in twenty four hours. Then reassess. See if you are ready to go back. The case won't disappear, no one is expecting to see you tomorrow and you'll be better able to work if you're not spending half your energy pretending to be fine instead of licking your wounds and going easy on yourself.

Ray was taking the kids to school. I hugged Maddie before they left. 'We've missed some bedtime reading recently, haven't we? I'll do double tonight.'

'Triple,' she said.

'Deal. You were snoring, you know,' I teased her.

'Was I?' Her eyes beamed.

'Like this.' I made outrageous snoring sounds.

'I was not,' she yelled, laughing.

'No, OK, you're right,' I said, 'that was Tom.'

'Huh! No way!' Tom objected.

'Does Ray snore?' Maddie said to me. Pointedly. The kids now knew we sometimes shared a bed. They must have absorbed the chilling of relations. The lack of affectionate gestures or kind words, the absence of a little light flirting or gentle sparring between us. They are like little Geiger counters, really.

'Snores like a pig,' I told her.

He didn't even grace me with a look.

'We could go shopping,' I suggested to Leanne. 'Get a couple of the things for your room.'

'It's really definite, then?' she asked. 'Have you talked to him?'

'It's definite,' I said, choosing not to answer the second question.

'Cool. I haven't got any money, though. I'll have to go to Jobcentre Plus, register here, then get on to the housing benefit.'

'Tomorrow. Let's do the fun stuff first,' I said. 'We can get a TV, too.'

'Maddie said they couldn't have a telly because they had broken it.' Leanne studied me.

'Yeah, well.' My agreement with Ray went straight out of the window. I seemed to be making a habit of disregarding his views: moving Leanne in, reinstating the TV. But it didn't seem unfair to me, not in the scale of things, not half so bad as his refusal to include me in his personal life. I wanted us to be sitting up till the early hours, chewing it all over. I wanted to be supporting him, listening as he worked through his confusion. Not cut off like someone who didn't matter, who didn't have a special, intimate place in his life.

We measured the windows in the flat and I explained to Leanne that we'd need different amounts of fabric depending on whether she wanted to pleated curtains on a rail like the existing ones or ones with a pole and rings across the top.

'I like these,' she said, and then looked troubled. 'Will that be more money?'

'Yes, but it won't break the bank.' Though the new telly might, I thought to myself.

Her reaction to Abakhan's material shop, a treasure trove of fabric piled in great bins and stacked in piles, much of it for sale by the pound weight, was all I had hoped for. I'd no idea if Leanne had any capacity for sewing, it didn't matter, really, but she loved rummaging around and kept getting distracted.

'I can make Lola a tiger outfit,' she hooted, holding up some stripy fun fur.

She had even more fun looking upstairs at all the trimmings, 'Check the feather boa! Maybe you need one of those for the old man.'

'He's not my old man,' I said. It just didn't sound right; like we were some old married couple.

'The old man,' she said, stressing the '*the*'. 'He's old, and he is a man, or am I missing something?' She cocked her head on one side, scrutinized me. 'So what's the story?'

I hesitated. 'It's complicated.'

'You saying I'm thick?' she challenged me. Oh, boy! The touchiness of teenagers.

'No,' I blew out, constructed an opening. 'His ex, Laura . . .'

'He was married?' she said.

'Girlfriend. She's had a baby. He's only just found out. It's thrown him.'

'So he's got a downer on you?'

'No,' I said.

She curled her lip. 'That's what it looks like from where I'm standing. He's nicer to the dog.'

I sighed. 'I want him to let me help, to talk about it. He's not very good at that. In fact, he's totally rubbish.' I moved aside to let someone past us. 'We thought Lola was Laura's baby at one point, that she had dumped her on us for Ray to look after.'

'I didn't dump her!' Leanne was all offence.

'Left her, then,' I said steadily.

She grimaced. 'You thought he might be the dad? Ewww! That is totally gross!'

'He can't be as bad as her real dad given everything you've told us.'

'You're right there,' she conceded easily enough. Her eyes roamed over the rolls of cloth and she twirled a strand of hair around her fingers. 'There,' she nodded, 'I like that gold one there.'

Material measured and bagged, I drove us to Ikea.

'Not been here,' she said, bending to get Lola out.

'Really?' I said. 'Once in a lifetime opportunity – never again. Least I bet that's what you say when we come out the other end.'

I was wrong. She loved it, and relished the slow parade through the furnished rooms upstairs which always drives me nuts. She wasn't gushing: she knew what she liked and what she didn't. 'That is mingin',' she said of one bedroom layout, 'give you a migraine, them colours.' But she loved the whole playing house, interior design thing. Of course she would. The local authority care homes Leanne had grown up in had been toxic places, brothels in effect, where she was at the mercy of staff who had managed to infiltrate the system for their own ends and maintained a regime of violence and abuse. No amount of toning colour schemes or cheery duvet covers would have mitigated the effects of that. Home had not been a refuge or a place of safety. The opposite.

I wondered if she had had a place of her own in the years since we last met. How long she remained homeless and on the run before she had found help with the project she mentioned in Leeds. I didn't ask. It was something I hoped she'd share in the fullness of time.

She chose a bedside lamp and a cot that would later adapt into a child's bed. I felt a little tingle of anticipation at the thought of the future rolling out before us, Lola growing up alongside Maddie, and hopefully Tom. A more dubious thought followed: was I replacing Ray and Tom with Leanne and Lola? Was that my real motive for offering them a home? An insurance policy for myself. Was it actually a selfish move – was I just using them? No, I told myself. OK there was an element of selfishness in there – I liked the idea of new people in the house, these new people, and the notion that the baby would be staying – but it didn't go anywhere near making up for the loss of Ray and Tom if it came to that.

'Meatballs,' I offered Leanne, feeling weary now we had emerged at the other end of the shopping experience and got through the tills.

She looked puzzled. I nodded to the restaurant. Her expression altered: a grin.

Leanne fed and changed Lola and we ate our meatballs – well she did; I had the herring. In the car park, after we had loaded the car, Leanne smoked a fag while I sang Lola to sleep.

I had managed to forget about work for several hours, then, as we were heading to our last port of call – Curry's, Leanne said, 'So who did beat you up, if it wasn't him?'

I must have flinched because she said, 'Was it him?' There was uncertainty and concern in her voice.

'No!' I insisted.

'Right,' she said disparagingly, as though she didn't believe me. She wasn't gonna leave it without an explanation.

'It's to do with work. Confidential, really,' I said. Hoping she would get the hint.

'Fine,' she grumbled, indicating my reticence was anything but. She sighed noisily and twiddled with her hair again. Her impatience was tangible. 'I'm not a kid,' she said after a couple of minutes.

'A conman,' I said, watching the traffic as we approached the big roundabout that I hated navigating. 'The sort of bloke who rips people off for a living. Really nasty piece of work.'

'You investigating him?'

'No.' I swore as somebody cut in front of me and I waited until we had got round the island and left it in one piece before explaining. 'No, but there was bad blood between him and someone else: a guy who was killed last year.'

'Murdered!' she said, surprised.

'Yes. They got someone for it but he retracted his confession. That's what I'm looking into. Anyway, the conman's name came up, I tried to trace him and he ambushed me outside my office.'

'Jeez, when?'

'Before you showed up yesterday,' I said.

'The bruises are still coming out,' she said. 'They'll get even worse.'

'Thanks for that,' I said.

'You OK, though?'

'Still a bit shaken up, really,' I admitted.

'You should be more careful,' she said solicitously.

I tried not to smile. 'I do self-defence,' I said. 'But he trapped me in the car. I couldn't get at him.'

'Tosser.' She shook her head.

Once we were in the car park at the electrical retailers I reminded her again that the television didn't need to be any bigger than the last one and if we saw a small model we would get it for her room; otherwise we could try Aldi, who often had cheap electronic deals. 'We're after a bargain,' I said.

We were in luck. They were clearing out display items. I found a flat screen for downstairs and a smaller one for Leanne. 'You can always trade up, once you're working,' I said.

It would be a big bite into my meagre savings but I wasn't going to let that ruin my day.

I was anticipating a full-on row with Ray once he saw what I'd done. Was I angling for it, perhaps? Something to get us exchanging words, even if they were heated, hostile ones.

If so my hopes were thwarted because as soon as we got in the house, he muttered that he was going out. He didn't say where and didn't give me chance to ask.

After tea, Leanne helped me set up the television. She was a lot more techno-savvy than I was: while I was still peering at the manual, she had installed the channels and the kids were jostling for positions next to her on the sofa.

'Remember,' I told them, 'any arguments about the telly and you come and get me. And any arguments about anything else, take them out of this room.'

By the time I'd done my promised triple stint of bedtime reading I was worn out but in a much healthier way than the day before. Doing something normal and domestic with Leanne had strengthened our relationship and redoubled my belief that offering her shelter was a good move. I'd proven to myself that life went on, normal humdrum life, and that Nick Dryden's assault had not taken that away from me. Spending some money was a bit of a boost as well, if I'm honest.

It's true that when I thought of returning to work the next day, I still felt burdened by it. The case was getting harder, not easier: the options seemed to be narrowing, funnelling me into a dead end. For the first time, I accepted that maybe I'd fail. That perhaps I was never going to find out who killed Charlie. That I'd end up letting down Libby, and Chloe and Damien – not able to get the conviction quashed or the investigation reopened. That would be awful but I had to be realistic. The police and the courts believed Damien Beswick was guilty. I didn't. But without proof my conviction wouldn't change anything.

EIGHTEEN

The weather moved in during the night. Winds bringing thunderous clouds and heavy downpours. In the early hours, I woke to the sound of rain scattering like shot on the window. Later, I heard Lola's muffled cries, from the floor above.

It was still teeming down when I got up, before daylight. I let Digger out and watched him from the kitchen window. When I went out to clear up his mess, I could see the light on in Leanne's bedroom, a rectangle of yellow glowing in the pitch of the roof.

'You were up early,' I said later. 'Lola have an early start?'

'She slept till eight.' Leanne frowned.

'I saw the light on.'

She flushed and gave a little shrug. 'I keep the light on,' she said.

I understood. Like Maddie, she was scared of the dark. For all of her street smarts, her prickly edge, Leanne was just a teenager, and one who'd survived nightmares. I didn't like to think what she had faced in the dark, the demons, the shadows that had tried to break her. She was still vulnerable.

I was ensconced in my office by nine. Stewing on the case. Picturing Libby finding Charlie, working backwards to Damien discovering the body, to Damien arriving in the village, to Charlie driving up, locking his car, opening the cottage. Was there someone there? Someone waiting in the dark shadows of the building with a knife. Or someone hot on his heels? Driving up the hill after him?

Something sparked in my head. And my pulse jumped in response. Valerie had no trouble keeping up with Charlie, but he was a fast driver – a reckless one, even. Libby had described how Charlie would overtake in the most dangerous of circumstances. *The traffic was slow moving*, Valerie said. But an impatient driver like that will speed up even if the rest of us are diligently keeping pace. They're the sort of people who cut in and out of queues, rev the engine and streak off as the lights change. I find them deeply irritating. There was no way Charlie Carter would have meekly sat in line in weekend traffic. My mind was racing; a tingle spread through my veins.

I checked something on the computer, looking up the model of Charlie's car, then took a deep breath and dialled Val's number, praying she'd be at home. I was lucky.

'I'm so sorry to bother you again,' I said, playing nice, 'but I wanted to double-check something that you said yesterday.'

She sighed noisily. 'What?'

'You said the traffic was moving slowly when you followed Charlie. Was there any reason: a traffic jam or an accident?'

'It was just busy,' she said shortly. 'It always is.'

'Could you see Charlie driving?'

'Yes,' she said firmly.

'You couldn't see his face – you were behind him. It was dark by that time. And his car, that model, had those darkened windows. It was his car,' I said with emphasis, 'but was *he* driving?'

My heart was thudding in my chest and I'd a thirst in my mouth.

'Of course,' she said with annoyance.

'Could someone else have been driving the car?'

Who? I'd already run out of suspects: not Nick Dryden, no hint of a road rage stranger, not Damien, not Libby. And Heather, the person with the strongest motive, had an unbreakable alibi. But I hadn't considered the other person who would be hurt by the break-up of Charlie's marriage: the other person who had cause to resent Libby and to stop Charlie abandoning his family. Alex Carter.

Had Alex killed Charlie? Had he discovered his father was going to leave, or that he was still seeing the 'other woman'? The possibility fizzed inside me like the fuse to a firework. How did it fit with the anomalies at the cottage? With the new things Damien had told me about?

The picture was garbled, a half-finished jigsaw, but I sensed a pattern there if I could only grasp it.

'Could it have been Alex?' I said to Valerie Mayhew.

It made sense, it would explain the driving: the boy hadn't even passed his test. Charlie was incapable of keeping to the speed limit. There was a moment's pause. Then she exploded. 'Don't be ridiculous! Alex was there when we left. I saw him with my own eyes *and*,' she emphasized the word, 'he was there when we returned. Which would be physically impossible if he'd been in the car. Why on earth would Alex be driving Charlie's car? These are people's lives you're messing with. If you bother me again, or contact Heather or Alex I will report you.' She cut the connection.

I swallowed, feeling as though I'd had my wrists well and truly slapped. I muttered various dark things about her. Could I have got it so wrong? If not Alex driving then who on earth could it have been?

My mind continued darting about trying to stitch bits of the story together. It was hard to make it mesh. A step at a time, I muttered to myself. Was there any way to prove that someone else had driven Charlie's car? The keys, I thought. Charlie's car keys had been inside the cottage when Damien got there.

Geoff Sinclair did not sound pleased to hear from me, either.

'I won't keep you,' I assured him. 'Charlie's car keys. Were they fingerprinted?'

'Yes. Nothing on them.'

'Isn't that odd?' I persisted, hope rising that I was on to

something now. 'Wouldn't you expect Charlie's prints to be on them?'

'He might have worn driving gloves.'

'Did he?'

Silence. I tried to collate what I knew about Charlie and driving: he enjoyed watching car racing; he was an impatient driver, drove too fast, fast enough to get speeding tickets quite frequently. None of it helped me second-guess whether he wore gloves to drive. I couldn't think of anyone who did. Only when it was cold, or if the car heater was on the blink as mine used to be.

'What's the interest in his keys?' Sinclair asked.

'Just an idea.' I considered saying more, telling Sinclair my latest 'wild theory' but hung back. It all felt raw and fragile, like the bones of a structure still knitting together. I was loath to say it aloud and have Sinclair shoot it down in flames.

'Anything else,' he said wearily, 'and the officer you want to talk to is DS Dave Pirelli – like the tyres.' There was no way of knowing whether Dave Pirelli would have an open mind but at least he hadn't already labelled me as someone with an overactive imagination.

'Thanks.'

My next call was to Libby.

'I've got a question about Charlie. It might sound a bit odd but did he wear driving gloves?'

She gave a little laugh. 'No. Half the time he wouldn't even wear gloves at work. His hands were a mass of cuts and calluses. Why?'

'There weren't any fingerprints on his car keys; it seems a bit odd.'

'Well, he never wore gloves,' she repeated. 'Hats, sometimes. He looked good in a hat.' Her voice was warm with affection.

'What sort of hats?'

'Not baseball caps, proper hats. He'd one like a yachtsman's, and a Panama for the hot weather, and one of those Australian bush hats.' I'd a vision of Rolf Harris with corks hanging off his brim. 'Quite a collection,' she said.

'Libby, I'm sorry to go over this again, but when you got to the cottage, Charlie . . . Did he have his coat on?' I could recall Damien's account: the plaid shirt, the blood.

'No, it was hanging up.'

'And did it look like he'd just arrived?'

'What do you mean?'

'Was there any sign that he'd been there for more than a couple of minutes. Anything?'

There was quiet as she thought about my question. Then she spoke slowly. 'His toolkit was there. And the heating was on,' she added. 'It was quite warm in there.'

My ears pricked up. It was cold when Damien was in there, so the heating must have come on in between his leaving and Libby arriving. 'The heating,' I said, 'was it on a timer?'

'Yes, like the one I've got at home? Why?'

'I'm just trying to get the sequence exactly right,' I explained. 'You texted Charlie to say you might be late. When was that?'

'About three,' she said.

'Did he reply?'

'No.'

My heart skipped a beat. 'Would he usually?' I asked.

Her voice changed: a thread of foreboding in it. 'Yes, mostly. Why?'

'I don't have all the answers yet, Libby.' There were still gaps, contradictions, puzzles.

'But you have some? I need to know.' She sounded intent.

'As soon as it's clearer, I'll ring you back. I promise.'

Everything Libby had told me supported the emerging theory I had. Charlie got to the cottage much earlier that November afternoon. In daylight. Much earlier than everyone had been led to believe. He had time to hang up his coat, bring in his toolkit, set the central heating to come on so the place would be warming up when Libby arrived. Then he was killed. Someone took his car and hours later, masquerading as Charlie, drove back to the cottage to make it look like Charlie was still alive. Creating an alibi for his wife Heather. Heather Carter must have known the car that they were following was not being driven by Charlie. Then who? Whichever way I threw the dice I got the same answer staring at me. Who else could that be but Alex? Something I'd already been told was impossible. Unless . . .

There was one final word of confirmation I needed but it meant speaking to Valerie Mayhew again.

'Just one more question, please,' I spoke in a rush, pleaded with her, gripping the phone, 'then I won't bother you again.'

'No. Enough's enough. And I've told Heather to have nothing more to do with you. I'm not prepared to countenance—'

I hurried on, ignoring the acid in her tone. 'Did you see Alex as soon as you got back to the house? Did you actually see him then or only later?'

The pause stretched out. I swallowed, the muscles in my back were stiff, my belly clenched with tension.

'Mrs Mayhew?'

'I could hear him. Heather went up to see him. He was still on his games.'

'And he came down later for tea?'

'Yes,' she agreed.

'What about Charlie? Did you see Charlie at the house when you first called for Heather?'

She didn't say anything. I felt a jolt of excitement, a flip in my stomach. I was right. 'Did you see Charlie?'

'What are you getting at?' Again she could not confirm it. I wasn't losing my marbles, I was on the right track.

I thought of Heather, the grieving widow. Her plausible performance when I'd first seen her after she'd had the letter from Chloe. And Alex, a typical shy teenager. One who'd had to bear the trauma of his dad's death.

'I think Alex drove the car,' I said. 'I think Charlie was already dead by then.' And you were a patsy, set up to seal their alibis. I didn't say that last bit out loud.

'This is ridiculous,' said Valerie. 'You're making a big mistake.' But there was more uncertainty than conviction behind her words.

Heather or Alex had killed Charlie, then both of them had been involved in the cover-up. Heather constructed the fake scenario of getting Valerie to help her trail her errant husband, Alex had driven Charlie's car to the cottage, creating a false alibi and using Valerie to seal the deal. Was Heather the killer? She was losing her husband to another woman. Sexual jealousy is a very powerful emotion. Perhaps she had got wind that Charlie was breaking his promise and sneaking off to see Libby. Perhaps she'd even been told the lie about Charlie going to the NEC for the weekend and seen through it, regurgitating it later for Valerie and the police. Or was Alex the one who killed Charlie? Possibly spurred on by his mother's distress. Had he been the one with the knife? My mind was cycling, stuck tracing a Mobius strip, trying to grasp the full picture.

The phone rang again. Had Valerie thought of something else? 'Hello?' I said.

'This is Heather Carter.'

The back of my neck prickled and I felt my stomach drop.

'Valerie rang me earlier.' Her voice was soft, troubled. 'She said you were asking questions about us, about Alex and me.'

I didn't confirm or deny it, just sat it out waiting to see what she wanted.

'I'd like a chance to talk to you, to try and clear things up.'

As if it was a little minor misunderstanding; something that could be ironed out, fixed by a little civilized discussion.

'You can talk to me now,' I told her.

'Not over the phone,' she said.

Was it a trap? There was no way I was going round to her place. If Heather had done what I thought she'd done then she would be desperate to stop the news getting out. That thought was followed swiftly by another: if Heather tried to hurt me it would be obvious to the whole world whodunnit and she'd be inviting arrest. She'd be stupid to try anything – and her ability to evade detection, presumably to think fast and smart under enormous pressure, to protect Alex and herself and persuade the policy of their innocence, showed she was far from stupid.

Nevertheless, I exercised caution. I wouldn't invite her into my space either but meet her somewhere neutral. Somewhere busy, in public where we could talk without people listening.

'Albert Square,' I told her. 'Outside the town hall, half past two.'

She thanked me and hung up.

I'd a sick feeling of apprehension about meeting Heather but it was tempered by a keen curiosity. My chest felt tight and my throat dry and I shivered, chilly even though I had the heating on.

Heather Carter was there before me; I saw her get to her feet from the bench where she was sitting and I raised an arm in acknowledgement. That hurt. I was still having to move gingerly to try and minimize the pain from Dryden's attack on me.

The storm had moved on by mid-morning and now the day was fine: wisps of cloud in a china-blue sky, the sun slanting across the cobbled square, caressing the honey-coloured stone of the town hall with golden light, everything washed clean by the rain.

As I'd hoped, the place was busy with people: office workers on late lunches eating sandwiches or smoking, a large party of oriental tourists, maybe Japanese or Chinese, following a tour guide over to the fountain at the far side of the square.

Heather and I had the bench to ourselves. Her forehead was furrowed with concern; I could see the tension in her shoulders, huddled as though she was cold in spite of the roll-neck sweater and brown suede jacket she wore.

I waited for her to speak, nervous myself, feeling faintly nauseous, but intrigued as to how she would play it.

'These . . .' She faltered, began again, her fingers worrying at each other. 'The things you've been implying – that we might have lied. I don't know how you've come up with that idea but it's a horrible mistake. I want to set things right.'

I didn't believe her, not for one second. If she and Alex were innocent, she'd not have given me the time of day. She'd more likely have gone to the police herself, to complain, and would never have invited me to meet with her. She was on a fishing trip, I thought, to see how much I knew, see how big a threat I was.

'You're wasting my time. I didn't come here to be fed more lies.' I got to my feet, ignoring the stab of pain in my calves.

'Please wait,' she said quickly. 'It's not what you think.'

I sat back down carefully. 'One of you killed Charlie,' I said quietly, 'then you covered it up.'

'No,' she insisted.

Across the square a man stepped into a taxi and the cab pulled away; the line of black taxis moved up the rank. A flock of pigeons rose and circled the square. A woman was taking photographs of the marble statue of Oliver Heywood, raised to the benefactor for his devotion to the public good.

'Either you or Alex were at the cottage earlier,' I carried on, 'and you constructed an alibi, making it look like Charlie was still alive much later in the day and exonerating yourselves. Damien Beswick was convicted on the strength of his false confession. He died in prison. He couldn't face another night, another day. He hung himself rather than go on. You knew he was innocent.'

'I loved Charlie,' she said, still denying any blame.

'And you were losing him,' I pointed out.

Her face flooded with colour and she turned her head away. A light breeze toyed with the curls on her head.

Another cab drove off. The photographer walked along to the bronze of Gladstone.

'What are you here for, Heather? What did you expect?'

'It's not all cut and dried,' she said. 'You talk as if you know everything and you don't. We had nothing to do with it.'

'I know enough to talk to the police,' I said.

'The police already investigated,' she said sharply. 'There are no grounds to do so again. You're just going to make a complete fool of yourself.'

'There's new evidence: evidence from Damien Beswick. It's all in my report. I think it's compelling.' At that stage I didn't even know whether Damien's evidence would be allowable, given he wasn't around to be tested on it. But I was banking on the fact that she wouldn't, either.

'What evidence?' She sounded perplexed.

I wasn't going to disclose any details. I didn't want to give her the ammunition. 'You're going to need a lawyer,' I said.

'I didn't do it,' she said simply.

I sighed, growing tired of her protestations. Her silence stretched out, then the bell in the town hall clock tower rang out once for quarter to three: a mournful toll. The pigeons wheeled and landed by the benches, scouring the cobbles for crumbs. They were a scrappy bunch: two had deformed feet and another had dull, bedraggled feathers.

I waited, counting silently to ten, preparing to leave her.

'It was an accident,' she whispered, 'a silly accident.'

'No reason for a cover-up, then,' I came back.

'He didn't mean it,' her voice trembled, 'it was self-defence.'

'Who?'

'Alex.' The word choked her.

I felt prickling as the hairs on my forearms rose.

'Charlie lost his temper. He flared up sometimes, it was frightening. He could be very violent. He went to hit Alex and Alex grabbed the knife. He was just trying to protect himself but Charlie tried to get it, he tripped. He fell.' She gave a shaky breath.

I tried to imagine the situation. Charlie yelling, Alex panicking, fearful, grabbing what was to hand. Charlie lunging and the sudden, irreversible horror as he fell. The blood. Alex rigid with shock, his father dying before his eyes. The terror at what he had done consuming everything else.

A car cut in front of another, swinging round the corner into the square. The blare of horns startled me.

'Where were you?' I asked.

'I wasn't there,' she said simply. 'Alex rang me: he was hysterical, terrified.'

'He didn't call an ambulance? Get help?'

'It was too late.' She shuddered beside me. Her face was etched with anxiety. 'Alex was petrified; he knew he'd be arrested, locked up. That's why he needed the alibi. If it had been me then no question . . . but my son.' Her voice quavered.

'His age,' I objected. 'The circumstances – they'd have been taken into account. If it was an accident or even self-defence he wouldn't be blamed.'

'What if they didn't believe him? He wouldn't hear of it and I couldn't risk it. I couldn't lose him as well.' She sniffed.

I watched a man, clutching a can, walk unsteadily to the Albert Memorial, settle down on the bottom step and lay a cap on the floor by his feet.

'What good would it do now?' she asked.

'You sacrificed another boy's life for Alex's,' I said.

She had no answer for me, her mouth worked with emotion. 'I came here to beg,' she said. 'Perhaps I was foolish—'

'Callous.' I couldn't keep quiet. Seeing Damien again, twisting in his chair, that sudden fleeting smile, the last glimpse I had of him as he lay his head on his arms. Defeated. I was determined to make her acknowledge the extent of the damage she'd done.

'But I had to protect Alex. He was all that I had left. He was so frightened. He's never been strong. He was terrified of Charlie.'

'Why was Alex there, at the cottage?' After all, I thought, Libby was due to turn up later. He might run into her. The three adults had tried to keep the state of play from Alex, not wanting to upset him before his exams. So why would Charlie have taken him there?

'Driving practice.' She stared at her nails. I saw the wedding ring on her finger. That she wore it still seemed monstrous. 'Alex was taking lessons. Charlie said Alex could drive out there; he was laying carpet and Alex was going to help him fit it.' She cleared her throat.

The flock of tourists disappeared up the steps into the main entrance of the town hall.

'So the phoney conference at the NEC – you invented that for the alibi?'

'No, that was true. Charlie had told us he was going on down there later that afternoon.'

'And how would Alex get home?'

'Charlie would drive him back to the main road on his way to the M6. There's a bus from there.'

How had they held it together? I wondered. Blood on their hands. Where had they found the resolve to enact the pantomime for Valerie Mayhew? To fake their reactions when the police came with tragic news? How on earth had a seventeen-year-old boy not betrayed the terror in his soul as he sat beside his mother and answered those mundane questions about the day?

And in the weeks that followed when they were informed of the arrest of a suspect, when they buried Charlie, when they went to court to hear Damien plea, how had they borne that secret?

'He nearly went mad.' Heather spoke as if she could hear my thoughts. 'He still has nightmares. He can't go to college. He couldn't survive in prison.' Anguish tore at her words.

'Nor could Damien.'

She looked away again. I was aware that she had ventured no apology for any of it: not a sorry for lying, for the miscarriage of justice, not a word of regret for Damien's suicide.

'Perhaps that would have happened anyway,' she said. 'By all accounts—'

'Don't you dare.' I felt anger sluice through me, my skin grow hot, my chest burn. I stood up. The taxi drivers were clustered outside their cabs, exchanging gossip, smoking, laughing on this fine autumn day.

'You'll destroy him,' she pleaded. 'For what? Have you no compassion?'

I walked away, across the setts, past the Albert Memorial, up along Princess Street where the wind was funnelled along the road, and the traffic swept past, unending, relentless.

NINETEEN

The bus cruised down Oxford Road, past the BBC and the universities, on through Rusholme and Fallowfield. I was dimly aware of the people paying, showing their passes, of those getting off, murmuring their thanks to the driver, of the mix of old and new buildings along the route. The weather was changing again, the sky darkening and there were the first fat drops of rain. But I was rerunning Heather's story, thinking that if I went over it often enough it might become comprehensible. I didn't dispute the facts of what she'd told me and they fitted with Damien's account, but the sheer scale of collusion, the amorality and audacity, the stone cold nerve that both of them had demonstrated was hard to swallow.

Not quite ready to face home and hearth, I went to the park when I got off the bus. In the little copse by the stream, where the path meanders and old frayed rope swings hang from the sturdier branches, I watched the sun slice beams through the crown of the trees and midges dance in their shadows. The air was rich here, redolent of sap and must and the heavy clay soil.

Libby needed to know what had happened, Chloe, too, and then Dave Pirelli, the police detective and Damien's lawyer. There was nothing to stop Heather denying her confession to me; in fact, if she was still hell bent on protecting Alex, she'd have to. Having come this far and with little sign of guilt or shame for her behaviour, she would probably stick to her original version of events. Had she really expected me to let it lie? For me to walk away and say no more about it? Did I have enough to convince the police to reopen the case? A hearsay confession from Heather, the recollections of a dead man: a darkened cottage, a cooling engine, a stranger hurrying down the hill. Could that possibly be enough?

Abi had walked the kids home and when I arrived back Maddie and Tom had been playing make-overs with Leanne. They'd raided my cosmetics and various kitchen items. Maddie had full-blown panda eyes and her hair had been backcombed and sprayed, forming clots and spikes, a sort of dragged-through-the-hedge look. In a stroke of genius, Leanne had suggested special effects to Tom, who had a scar across one cheek (lipstick, eye pencil, peanut butter and cornflakes), a moustache and a tattoo on his arm. Not to be left out, Baby Lola sported cat's whiskers and a black nose.

I wasn't unaware of the contradictory position I held. On the one hand I was intent on making the truth known about Alex's attack on his father and the ensuing cover-up engineered by his mother and determined to see justice done – for Charlie, for Libby, for Damien and his family. On the other I was sure that my decision not to reveal the truth about Leanne's past crime and in effect to help her evade prosecution was the right one. Alex had unintentionally killed his father in a messy argument; Leanne had intentionally taken a life in an act of revenge, in the midst of a terrifying encounter, hitting back at one of the men who had orchestrated abuse on a brutal scale.

The process of law can be a clumsy tool but while I thought Leanne would only have suffered further at its hands, I really believed there'd be understanding and clemency for Alex. If only he had admitted to the terrible accident immediately. His mother's counsel had been disastrous, distorting everything and trapping them both in a tragic lie.

Why had Heather been so intent on covering up? Had it not been the accident that she described? Self-defence, she had said at one point. Charlie had been violent – lunging at the boy. But if that wasn't the whole truth, if Alex deliberately attacked his father then Heather's actions after the death made a lot more sense.

I'd rung Libby and asked her to come round to my office. I wanted to tell her what I'd learnt in person. I told Leanne that Ray would soon be home if she could hold the fort till then – I'd be an hour or so.

Even with an umbrella, I got wet walking the short stretch to work. The rain drummed on the cars parked along the roadside and gushed along the gutters. It spattered the leaves on the trees and bounced off the paving stones.

In my office the Tupperware on the window sill was catching the drops from the leak in the narrow basement window frame: plop, plop, plop. I turned up the heating to take the chill off the room, made fresh coffee and rang Dave Pirelli. He was in, though rushed. But I impressed on him that what I had to tell him was extremely serious and wouldn't wait. He couldn't cancel his meetings that day but promised to see me first thing in the morning. I was thankful he hadn't given me the brush-off or told me not to waste police time – both responses I have had from detectives in the past.

How might Libby react? I was nervous, having second thoughts. The truth would be a huge shock. Might it not be easier to fudge what I'd learnt and leave it as it was? If and when the police took action they could answer Libby's questions. But I owed her: she'd hired me to do my best and expected an honest account from me. Could she handle it? Thinking about Libby and how she had conducted herself reassured me: she had survived the pressure of suspicion when the police first began the enquiry; she hadn't gone haring off to Chloe Beswick when she got the letter about Damien's conviction but brought me in to check it out; she had coped with me finding merit in Damien's position with good grace and had now gone so far as to reverse her opinion and join Chloe Beswick in asking for further police investigation. She had done all this after finding Charlie violently killed, and in the midst of her shock and grief. In the past year she had lost her lover, their future together and had borne his baby. The latter in itself can be enough to make a woman slightly deranged for a good while, going by my own experience. She had kept her business going, too. Libby was strong enough to take the news and sorted enough not to do anything stupid. I'd a box of tissues handy in case of tears – and a bottle of brandy in the filing cabinet, in the best private-eye tradition.

Libby shook the rain off her coat and I told her to leave it on the hooks in the hall. She'd brought Rowena in with her; the baby was dozing in her car seat.

We sat on the sofa downstairs in my office. She picked up on the atmosphere straight away. 'What's happened to your face?'

'Nick Dryden warning me off.'

'Oh, my God!'

'But he's not involved with what happened to Charlie. He got the wrong end of the stick: thought I was spying for his creditors or the authorities. And I got the wrong end of his temper.'

'Have you reported it?'

I shook my head. 'I'm going to let it go. Too complicated. I don't ever expect to hear from him again. But I've got other news. It's going to be a big shock,' I warned her, 'I'm sorry.'

She drew herself up in preparation and regarded me solemnly; a wary look hooded her eyes.

I repeated what Heather had told me, sticking to the bare bones of the confrontation. Her eyes filled with tears and she didn't say anything for a few moments after I'd finished speaking. Then she rubbed her hand across her forehead. 'So, the alibi, and the things that Damien remembered – how does it all fit together?'

'Here's what I think. After it had happened, Alex rang his mother, probably hysterical, panicking. She told him to come back, to drive his father's car home and she worked out a way to create an alibi.'

Libby gave a sad smile. 'Charlie always said she was clever.'

'Well, when Alex got back they must have rehearsed what to do. Then she rang Valerie. Gave her the story about wanting to catch Charlie out, how he'd told her he was off to the NEC but she thought he was cheating on her, breaking their understanding and going to meet you.'

'That wasn't so far from the truth,' Libby admitted.

'The best lies run close,' I said. 'So, Valerie sees Alex when she calls for Heather. Alex then goes upstairs. He has his games console on. Heather makes a show of calling out goodbye to Charlie or maybe she even goes up and pretends to say goodbye to him. Some gesture to persuade Valerie that Charlie has not left the house, yet. Valerie never sets eyes on Charlie but she's tricked into thinking he's there. Then Heather and Valerie wait down the road in Valerie's car. When Charlie's car appears exiting the Carters' drive they follow. It's easy to keep up as he's going so slowly; that's because Alex is driving and he's still a learner.'

Libby stared at me. 'The opposite of Charlie, who drove like a maniac.'

'Precisely.'

'And she wouldn't be able to tell it was him because of the tinted windows,' Libby pointed out.

'Yes, and don't forget it was twilight. Now, the women didn't want Charlie to notice them so Valerie even hung back at one point to let a car get between them. When Charlie's car turns off towards the cottage, Heather plays the wounded wife. Valerie and Heather drive back home to the house in Hale. It sounds like Alex is still gaming upstairs, making a right racket. Heather complains to her friend and goes up and asks him to turn it down a bit. But he's not there; it's all a ploy. Meanwhile, Alex reaches the cottage and parks Charlie's car in the drive. He locks the car. He has to go inside and leave the car keys. When they are later found there are no fingerprints on them so he must have wiped them clean.'

'The knife?' Libby asked me.

'I don't know,' I admitted. 'It was never found – he must have got rid of it.'

Libby shook her head, covering her mouth with her hand. Distressed, I imagined, at the harrowing thought of Alex in that gruesome situation.

'Alex walks down the hill, passing Damien. He gets the bus back as close as he can then walks the rest of the way home. He sneaks upstairs and is there when Heather serves dinner. And they wait for the police to call.'

Libby sat there stunned, hands to her temples, gazing in the direction of Rowena, though I don't think she was actually seeing her daughter or taking anything in from the room, from the present. Finally she moved her hands, straightened up and turned to me. 'I don't believe it,' she said.

'It's hard to credit,' I agreed.

'No, not the cover-up: the fight. Charlie wasn't like that, he was a very patient man. He never lost his temper.'

'With you,' I said.

'In general. Honestly, the only time he got wound up was when he was driving.'

'Maybe that was it,' I suggested. 'Alex was driving out there with him to get some practise. If Alex was going slowly, making mistakes, then Charlie would find it hard to keep calm. He'd be pretty wound up when they got there, then if Alex did something to make it worse . . .'

Libby shook her head. 'No,' she insisted, 'Charlie would never have lost it like that. He'd never lay a finger on that boy.'

'So, what Heather said about the fight . . .'

'Bullshit,' Libby said succinctly.

'So was it something more sinister? Not an accident.' But a boy that age. Where would such violence come from? 'Alex – there was never any suggestion he was disturbed in any way?' I asked her.

'No. He was a bit shy. Sensitive. Stuck in his room, Charlie said, always on his computer. He didn't have many friends; Charlie worried about that. Do you think Alex found out about us?'

'It's a helluva leap from that to picking up a knife.' I imagined Alex, chaotic, confused, the blade in his hand, accusing his father, one fateful move. Talking to his mother, fleeing the scene, shock descending. Then the purgatory of driving back there. The cottage in the dark. Having to open that door. Feel the presence. Gag on the smell of death. The frantic scurry down the hill to the bus, passing Damien on his way up.

Ice froze in my veins; my heart grew heavy, a weight solid in my chest. 'Oh, God.'

'What?' Libby sat forward, alert to the urgency in my voice.

'He can't have taken the bus home,' I said. 'They're only every half hour and Damien had just got off the bus. Damien ran back to the bus stop after he'd stolen Charlie's wallet. He waited for the next bus and he was alone at the bus stop.'

Libby shook her head, slowly. 'More lies? What's going on, Sal?'

'I don't know. Damien heard a car start up. Maybe Alex drove another car home.'

'But you said he drove Charlie's car; he couldn't drive two cars.'

There was hammering on the front door.

'I'm sorry,' I said to Libby. 'I won't be a minute.'

It was Alex Carter, his clothes drenched with rain, his hair plastered to his head, shivering, looking younger than his years, hunted, haunted.

TWENTY

'She came to see you?' he asked. His voice shook.

I swallowed. 'Come in,' I told him.

He stepped into the hall, his hands rammed in his pockets, shoulders hunched. Shivering still, his face red from the weather. 'She won't tell me what's happening. But I know she came to see you: the number was on the phone.'

'You should go home,' I said gently, 'talk to your mum.'

'I asked her.' He raised his voice in frustration. 'She won't talk to me! Is she in trouble?'

Oh, Alex. The naivety of the question was hard to fathom. He'd obviously no idea how much I already knew. I formulated a neutral reply; the last thing I wanted was him freaking out on me. 'It's likely that the conviction of Damien Beswick was unsound. The police will be examining new evidence; they may reopen the investigation.'

'They can't!' he breathed, his eyes fixed on me.

I didn't speak.

'I can't bear it,' he said. He slid down the wall put his head in his hands, his knees bent up.

'Shall I ring her, Alex?' I asked. 'She can come and pick you up?'

The reedy wail of Rowena crying came from below. Alex

frowned, looking confused, and shook his head at my offer. 'No,' he mumbled. He circled his knees with his arms, his head buried.

'It was an accident,' I said.

He raised his head to look at me, his face twisted in disbelief. 'She told you?'

I nodded.

'Why?' he said with horror. 'Why did she tell you? We promised—' he was too distraught to continue.

I rushed to calm him. 'She wanted to explain, I think, that it had been an accident.'

'She said no one would believe her,' Alex whispered. His lips were swollen and red, the skin flaking. 'That she'd be in prison for years. I don't want her to go to prison!'

My skin crawled and adrenalin coursed through me like toxin. I crouched down. 'For lying?' I asked softly. I could feel my heart in my throat.

He stared at me, misery on his face, dull confusion. 'No, for what she did.'

My tongue stuck to the roof of my mouth; I tried to swallow. 'The accident?'

The stairs creaked and Libby appeared, Rowena in her arms. Alex glanced over at her, almost indifferent. I stood, crossing to her to try and prevent the encounter but I hadn't reckoned on Libby's determination.

'Alex?' she said.

'Who are you?'

'Libby.'

He froze, the colour draining from his face. 'That was why they were arguing,' he said, 'because of you.'

'Arguing?' asked Libby.

'If you hadn't been—'

'The accident,' I interrupted, catching Libby's eye, signalling this was important. 'It was Heather.'

Alex looked at Libby, then back to me. 'What are you on about?' His eyes glittered. Drops of rain trickled from the ends of his hair.

'Heather told Sal it was you.' Libby was trembling slightly; it was just possible to see. 'You were with Charlie, there was an argument, Charlie went for you, you were scared, you picked up the knife. Charlie stumbled, he fell on the knife.'

'You're lying.' He scrambled to his feet, his eyes darting wildly, seeking escape.

'Alex,' I put out an arm, trying to still him.

'She'd never do that,' he shouted. But the truth had already hit him. He turned suddenly, howling, slapped his palms against the wall then slammed his head against it. The sound was sickening. He did it again. I grabbed his arms, shocked at how skinny they were and the feel of his bones, and pulled him away, turned him to face me. Keeping my voice steady, I said, 'Alex, sit down, sit down.'

He obeyed. Sat on the floor again.

Libby was fighting back tears, her face raised, neck stretched, eyes blinking. One hand rhythmically patting Rowena's back, keeping the baby quiet.

'I'm sorry,' I told him.

'You believed her?' he asked, injured, his voice breaking.

I didn't answer him but asked a question of my own. 'After you drove back to the cottage, you left your dad's car on the drive. How did you get home?'

'In mum's,' he said quietly. 'She'd parked on the hill.' He was crying now, silently, the tears coursing down his cheeks.

'A Mondeo?' I asked. He dipped his head. The car Damien had passed going up the hill, casing it for easy access to valuables, and the engine he'd heard starting up. And Alex was the man he'd passed, the one out of breath, carrying a rucksack. I recalled the shift in Sinclair's face when I'd mentioned the cars. He must have made the connection, then. Known it was the same make as Heather Carter's. But he'd said nothing. Did he dismiss it as a coincidence or was he past caring? Unwilling to contemplate the miscarriage of justice that had occurred.

'Were you carrying anything?' I said.

'Dad's rucksack,' he said with difficulty. 'She'd put the knife in an old curtain. I had to leave it in one of those bins at the supermarket. I can't go home,' he blurted out, fear making his voice squeak. 'I'm scared.' His mouth trembled. 'I'm so scared.' He began to rock, a desperate feral motion and he bit at his hand. I put my hand on his shoulder, trying to ease his panic.

Heather had driven out there to confront her husband about his affair. They argued, she stabbed him, either intentionally or accidentally, then drove his car home and forced her son to help create the alibi. Now that the truth was bubbling to the surface she was prepared to name Alex as the killer. Ruthless, that's how Nick Dryden had described Heather, something I'd dismissed at the time, but a label she certainly deserved. Not only had she destroyed her son by pressing him to enact the ghastly pantomime to save her skin, but as the cover-up threatened to unravel she had no qualms at betraying her only child. Of course, she still probably clung to the hope that nothing would change, that I couldn't prove anything and that none of the authorities would take an interest in pursuing things any further.

But she hadn't reckoned on Alex, driven by terror and desperate to know why his mother had contacted me. Alex, driven to breaking point and finally revealing a much more plausible version of events.

'Alex,' said Libby, 'Heather claimed Charlie used to lose his temper. That he was violent. That he hit you. He never did that, did he?'

Alex shook his head slightly. 'I miss him,' he sobbed, wiping his nose on his sleeve.

'He was a good man,' said Libby.

'He was leaving us, though,' Alex cried.

'He was leaving her, not you,' said Libby. 'He loved you.'

Alex moaned, rolled his head back against the wall, his mouth stretching with tears.

'He'd agreed to stop seeing me,' Libby went on, 'until you'd done your exams. We didn't want to make it hard for you. And after that we hoped that you'd stay with us some of the time. He really loved you. It was my fault he lied to your mum that day. I wanted to meet up, to tell him I was pregnant. I'm so sorry.'

Alex stared at her.

'This is your sister,' Libby said, 'Rowena.'

Alex looked away, weeping now, his shoulders shuddering.

When he sounded a little calmer, I spoke. 'You need to talk to the police, tell them everything. OK?'

He nodded numbly. 'I didn't want to do it, but Mum said we had no choice—'

'She was your mother. People will understand. Just tell the truth.'

'I don't want to see her.' He grabbed my wrist, shivering. 'Don't let her near me. Please.'

'I promise.'

Alex's face glazed over, an expression of blank defeat, of desolation on it. He continued to rock, making a little moaning sound in the back of his throat. Whimpering. The sound of someone broken.

I hung on the phone until someone agreed to interrupt Dave Pirelli in one of his meetings. Then I gave him the option: did he want to come and arrest Alex Carter or should I call 999? I also warned him the boy was traumatized and would need medical attention and that on no account should his mother have any access to him.

They came with lights and sirens on. Some of the neighbours braved the rain to gawp and whisper as Alex was taken from the house and put into the patrol car. Dave Pirelli had the gist of the story from me and another car had been despatched to arrest Heather. I would be contacted in due time to make a full statement, as would Libby.

When they had gone, I turned to Libby. I felt drained, hollowed out, my blood too thin, my bones weak. 'I don't know about you,' I said, 'but I could do with a proper drink.'

She nodded. 'Thought you'd never ask.'

Downstairs again with Libby and Rowena I poured two generous measures. The brandy scorched my throat and belly and I felt my neck loosen, a sensation of heat spread along my limbs.

'Do you think it was an accident?' Libby asked me.

'No,' I said quietly.

She tilted her head, inviting me to elaborate.

'Heather would have tried to get help, dialled 999. You just would. She's not stupid. If it had been an accident the evidence would have backed her up but she knew it wouldn't. I don't think she set off for the cottage intending to harm Charlie. If she'd planned his death she could have come up with something less messy. She went to challenge him and she lost her temper, a moment's madness, a single blow.'

Libby drained her glass. 'How did the pair of them cope with it? Murdering someone. Knowing that they'd done that day after day, week after week. It must have been hell.'

'Yes. Well, you saw the state of Alex.'

Libby snorted, disgusted. 'She'll get life?'

'God, I hope so.'

'And Alex?' She pulled the elastic band from her ponytail and ran her hands through her hair.

'Who knows? His age will work in his favour, and his co-operation now.' I twisted my glass, watched the amber liquid spin and shimmer. 'It's too late for Damien, though.'

'What a mess.' She refastened her hair. 'You'll tell Chloe?'

'Yes.'

'In your report,' Libby referred to the document I had prom-ised her, 'will you put in how it all happened, as far as you can tell, all the stuff that Damien told you, the times and everything?'

'Yes, of course,' I said.

'It's like I need to go over it, get it all fixed in my mind. I did that before when they convicted Damien. Does that sound weird, creepy?'

'No, I understand.' I'd had the same reaction to traumas in my own life. Absorbing the facts, revisiting them again and again, was a way of coming to terms with the emotions.

Libby and Rowena had gone. I'd be expected home but I wasn't fit company. The light was fading, the sky turning charcoal. A new moon, blurred by cloud, glowed above. The park was deserted. The football pitch was waterlogged already and some of the footpaths flooded. I walked at first, my legs stiff and aching from the bruises, then began to speed up until I was running at full pelt, fighting through the pain. The rain stung my face and hands, creeping down the back of my neck, soaking through my trousers. I increased my stride, felt the stretch in my calves and thighs, and the cold, damp air suck in and out of my lungs until my windpipe felt raw and my heart pounded in my skull. Running because I was sad and sickened and because I was alive with blood coursing through my veins and love and fear and hope in my heart.

* * *

Chloe's house was busy again when I called round early the following day. The funeral was set for that Friday and half the neighbourhood seemed to be involved in planning the arrangements.

'Can we talk in private?' I asked her.

'Upstairs.'

We went into her bedroom. She sat on the bed and pointed me to a wicker chair.

'Have you heard from the police?' I asked her.

She shook her head. 'Why?'

'They'll be reopening the investigation.'

'Honest? How come?' Her brow creased.

I told her. As she listened, she played with a teddy bear, bending its limbs, positioning it; something to keep her hands busy, her face mobile with emotion.

When I was done, she shook her head and put the bear down on the bed beside her. 'That bitch,' she said, her eyes glittery with tears. 'That bloody bitch.'

I couldn't disagree.

I tried letting Geoff Sinclair know what I'd found out, maybe wanting a little recognition that I hadn't been completely barking. But whenever I called, his answerphone was on. It's not the sort of information you leave on voicemail. Later, I learnt he'd gone into a hospice and died very soon after. I don't know if he ever heard that Heather Carter had been charged with murder or that her son Alex had been taken into psychiatric care, unfit to plead to charges of being an accessory.

I hoped that Libby would heal in time, that she'd meet someone new and build a life with him and her daughter. I couldn't pass a marquee without wondering about her, and what she would tell Rowena about her father Charlie. How do you tell your child that their father was murdered? That jealousy about you was a big part of the reason? And that another man, an innocent man, died in prison after falsely confessing? How much do you reveal? How long do you keep silent? When do you tell them? There can never be a good time for such shocking disclosures so how do you choose the moment? And how do you cope with the distress and the anguish that will result?

The day the truth came out, the day Alex turned up on the door-step of my office, I arrived home after my run in the park, sodden through, splashed with mud and grime and intent on having it out with Ray. Life was too short to be mucking about and I wouldn't stand for another minute of his prevaricating. We were in this together or it was over.

They were all in the kitchen.

Leanne gawped at me. 'Did you fall in?'

'Can you take the kids, Leanne,' I said tightly. 'Take them out for a bit.'

'It's raining,' she complained.

'It's easing off,' I said.

'It's dark,' Maddie said.

'There are street lights.' I pulled a damp twenty-pound note from my pocket and gave it to Leanne. 'Here – buy them tea or something. Left at the main road – there are places down in Didsbury.'

'We've had tea,' Maddie said.

'Have it again,' I snapped. 'Have pudding.'

'Cool.' Tom grinned.

'I'm not sure—' Ray finally chipped in.

'I am.' I glared at him. 'Go,' I said to Leanne.

Leanne's eyes flicked between us. 'Right,' she announced. 'Last one ready's a muppet.'

The kids flew out to the hall, giggling and Leanne scooped Lola up and carried her out. I stood, my back against the counter, arms folded, waiting for the sound of the front door closing behind them. Water seeped from the bottom of my trousers, forming pools on the floor. My thighs and neck felt clammy from the damp.

Ray didn't speak. The air between us sang with tension. I noticed my toes pressing against the floor, my back held rigid.

I heard the door slam.

'So,' I said, 'do you want to go first?'

He shuffled in his seat. 'Not really,' he said. I bit down on my temper. He looked my way. 'Your face,' he said, his expression opening with concern.

Top marks for observation, I thought sourly. 'Don't change the subject,' I said. 'You and me . . . stuff happens, Ray: babies, surprises, setbacks, things change. We don't have to let it destroy us.'

He gave an awkward shrug.

'Or is that the plan? You close down on me, cut me off. You sulk, you refuse to talk.' My voice was rising. 'You're so selfish – you never consider what it's like for me. It makes me feel helpless and needy and I hate it. I really hate it.' I was practically shouting, trying not to cry. I paced across the floor. 'I want to be with you but I don't know—'

He stood up, came closer.

'Don't touch me.' I raised a hand to ward him off.

'I love you, Sal.'

'Don't. I'm angry. I can't be angry when you, if you—' I was crying.

He raised his hand to mine and grabbed it; his was warm, large. 'I'm sorry. I'm so sorry. Come here.'

'No.' Like a child.

He kissed my eyelids, my mouth, hugged me close. 'We'll work something out. I don't want to lose you. Lose this. Everything's a mess at the moment but we'll find a way, yeah?'

'I hate you,' I told him.

'I know.'

'I really hate you.'

'Yes, I know.' He kissed my neck and ran his hand through my wet hair, gripped my head, kissed me again, his lips firm and warm where mine were still cold, his tongue smooth.

'You have to let me in,' I said. 'You have to share things with me. It won't work otherwise.'

'I know, I will. I promise, Sal.' He kissed me. 'Come upstairs,' he whispered.

'I'm hungry,' I sniffed.

'It'll keep. Come on.'

I was getting dizzy, my body responding, my breasts tingling, my belly hollow. I let him walk me to the door, guide me up the stairs, stopping to kiss, into his room.

'I still hate you.'

'You said.'

He peeled off my clothes, then his own. Lowered me into bed. I closed my eyes and let go, spinning and swimming and dancing. Sensations overwhelming me, crowding out thought and logic and memory. Stopping time.